Greek Paradise Escape

Travel from the comfort of your armchair with Jennifer Faye's brand-new trilogy!

Nestled on a private Greek island, the exclusive Ludus Resort is the perfect escape for the rich and famous. But to the staff who work there, it's home.

Manager Hermione's job has been a lifeline since losing her home and family, so when new owner Atlas plans to sell, sparks fly between them!

Beach artist Indigo is new to the resort and has already caught the eye of one of its VIP guests, the Prince of Rydiania...

Concierge Adara spends her days fulfilling guests' wishes. Might it be time her own romantic dreams came true?

Make your escape to beautiful Ludus in
Greek Heir to Claim Her Heart

And continue your journey with Indigo's and Adara's stories, coming soon!

Dear Reader,

This book was created during the pandemic, a time when the only escape was an armchair vacation. For me, it meant this trip could be as glamorous and fantastical as my imagination would allow. And who wouldn't want to visit a sunny private Greek island for a Valentine's ball, no less?

Well, now that you ask, my hero, that's who. Security expert and CEO Atlas Othonos doesn't want to visit Ludus Island and its luxury resort... even though he now owns it. Because dealing with the island means coming to terms with his painful past, and that's the last thing he wants. Atlas is determined to sell the resort to the first buyer.

Hermione Kappas has gone from a state of homelessness to being the manager of one of the world's finest resorts. In the process, the employees have become her makeshift family. But when the owner unexpectedly dies, the resort's future is at stake.

One stormy night, Atlas's and Hermione's lives collide and a friendship is born. But in the light of day, everything changes when identities are revealed. Atlas is there to destroy Hermione's world, but she's not going down without a fight.

Happy reading,

Jennifer

Greek Heir to Claim Her Heart

—

Jennifer Faye

H HARLEQUIN

Romance

H HARLEQUIN®

Romance™

Recycling programs for this product may not exist in your area.

ISBN-13: 978-1-335-40698-9

Greek Heir to Claim Her Heart

Copyright © 2022 by Jennifer F. Stroka

All rights reserved. No part of this book may be used or reproduced in any manner whatsoever without written permission except in the case of brief quotations embodied in critical articles and reviews.

This is a work of fiction. Names, characters, places and incidents are either the product of the author's imagination or are used fictitiously. Any resemblance to actual persons, living or dead, businesses, companies, events or locales is entirely coincidental.

This edition published by arrangement with Harlequin Books S.A.

For questions and comments about the quality of this book, please contact us at CustomerService@Harlequin.com.

Harlequin Enterprises ULC
22 Adelaide St. West, 41st Floor
Toronto, Ontario M5H 4E3, Canada
www.Harlequin.com

Printed in U.S.A.

Award-winning author **Jennifer Faye** pens fun, heartwarming contemporary romances with rugged cowboys, sexy billionaires and enchanting royalty. Internationally published, with books translated into nine languages, she is a two-time winner of the *RT Book Reviews* Reviewers' Choice Award. She has also won the CataRomance Reviewers' Choice Award, been named a Top Pick author and been nominated for numerous other awards.

Books by Jennifer Faye

Harlequin Romance

Wedding Bells at Lake Como

Bound by a Ring and a Secret
Falling for Her Convenient Groom

The Bartolini Legacy

The Prince and the Wedding Planner
The CEO, the Puppy and Me
The Italian's Unexpected Heir

Snowbound with an Heiress
Wearing the Greek Millionaire's Ring
Her Christmas Pregnancy Surprise
Fairytale Christmas with the Millionaire

Visit the Author Profile page
at Harlequin.com for more titles.

Praise for
Jennifer Faye

"A fantastic romantic read that is a joy to read from start to finish, *The CEO, the Puppy and Me* is another winner by the immensely talented Jennifer Faye."

—*Goodreads*

CHAPTER ONE

CHANGES WERE AFOOT.

Changes that didn't bode well for the immediate future.

Hermione Kappas wanted to be optimistic, but at the moment she was too tired. She was the general manager of the exclusive Ludus Resort. As she'd settled into her position this past year, she thought at last her life would be peaceful and predictable—two things she hadn't had growing up. And they had been for a while, but as quick as the flip of a coin everything had once more changed.

On this particular Monday evening, darkness had come early. She yawned as she gathered her things. She hated working this late. Thankfully it was a rare occurrence.

On her way to her car, she paused in the resort's spacious lobby. "How are things going, Titus?"

The nighttime desk clerk looked up. His gaze rose over the rim of his reading glasses. His older face, trimmed with a gray mustache, lit up with a friendly smile. "It's another quiet evening, just the way I like them." He removed his glasses. Concern reflected in his eyes. "You've been working late a lot recently."

She nodded. "I have been. I hope this evening is the end of it."

She'd been coordinating all of the requested information for the independent auditors. Now that the resort's owner had unexpected died, the resort's future was uncertain. And an audit was being conducted.

She hadn't been privy to the details of the will—only the part about her having the authority to keep the resort in operation until the estate was finalized, whatever that meant. She just did as instructed by the resort's legal team.

Titus nodded in understanding. "I'll miss chatting with you each evening, but I'm sure you're anxious to have life return to normal. Be careful out there. It's an ugly night."

"I will. Good night."

She paused at the front door and stared out at the pouring rain. With it being winter, she longed for just a little snow. In the northern part of Greece where she'd grown up, there was snow in February but down here in the south, the snow was replaced by periodic rain.

So be it. It wasn't like she'd melt. She pushed open the door. Once she stepped outside, the wind immediately caught her unzipped jacket. She grabbed the flaps and held them closed. When she reached the edge of the portico, she ran across the garden area to the nearby parking lot.

The rain fell in large drops, flattening her bangs and soaking her clothes. She hurled herself into the car. Wet and disheveled, Hermione sat in the driver's seat. As she wiped the wetness from her face, the raindrops pounded on the roof.

Hermione loosened her hair from the French twist at the back of her head and finger-combed her long hair. She leaned her head back against the seat and closed her eyes, letting the constant rap-a-tap-tap of the rain lull her into a state of relaxation. After being hunched over her desk since early that morning, her body ached.

With a sigh, she started the car and set off for the ferry that would transport her to the mainland. She couldn't wait to get home. There were some leftovers in the fridge so she wouldn't even have to prepare dinner. She could even eat in bed. The tempting thought had her pressing harder on the accelerator.

Just then there was a brilliant flash of lightning. It lit up the entire sky as though it were daytime again. A crack of thunder rumbled through the car. Then as though the heavens had opened up, the rain came down even harder and faster. The car slowed to a crawl. She increased the speed of the wipers as she squinted, trying to see the roadway.

A chill of apprehension raced down her spine,

leaving a trail of goosebumps in its wake. In the glow of the dashboard lights, her knuckles shone as she clutched the steering with both hands. As the wipers failed to keep up with the deluge of rain, she leaned forward, trying to see better.

A blur of white light blinded her. This time it wasn't lightning. It was a constant light and getting brighter. Headlights? Was there a vehicle headed toward her?

Her foot tramped the brake.

The weather was foul.

Just like his mood.

Atlas Othonos braked as a branch crashed onto the roadway in front of him. Luckily the road from the ferry to the Ludus Resort was deserted. He carefully wheeled around the debris and continued on his way. The strong winds pushed against the small car as though trying to shove him off the road.

Why hadn't he checked the weather forecast before deciding it was a good idea to pick up his brand-new car today of all days? He groaned in frustration. Weren't Greek islands supposed to be sunny and warm year-round?

The truth of the matter was that he didn't want to be on this small island—even though by some ironic twist of fate, it was all his. He owned an island—an exclusive island—the playground for the rich and famous. And he didn't want it. He didn't want any part of it. The sooner he could rid himself of it, the better.

His estranged mother, Thea as he called her, had died nearly two months ago. Not having seen her since he was young, he refused to acknowledge any feeling about her passing. Was that wrong? Perhaps.

Since it took Thea's attorneys a while to track him down in the States, the funeral was over before he knew what had happened. It was for the best. But the fact that she'd left everything in her will to him was not for the best. Not at all.

He'd dragged his heels as long as he could. The attorneys warned him the longer he took to sell the resort, the greater the chance of the business running into trouble. The only catch to selling the place was that he needed to oversee the estate.

The more he thought about it, the faster he drove. He'd worked so hard to avoid any of this, and in the end, he was to spend the next two weeks on the island going through his mother's personal finances and belongings. The thought twisted his gut up into a tight knot.

Atlas squinted, trying to make out the road. With the rain coming down in sheets, it was hard for him to see.

A flash of lightning or was that of headlights? Definitely headlights. They were headed straight toward him. They weren't slowing down. And they weren't moving over.

His body tensed.

He swerved.

His foot stomped the brakes. The tires slid forward over the wet pavement. He cut the steering wheel hard to the right. The car wouldn't respond. There was too much water on the road. His heart lodged in his throat. The car kept careening forward.

His body stiffened for the impact.

His car slid off the roadway and went down a small embankment. It finally slowed to a stop. With the windshield wipers rapidly swishing back and forth, he stared out into the darkness. He didn't spot the other car. Where were they?

He put the car in reverse. He pressed on the accelerator. The engine revved but the car didn't budge. Not about to give up, he tried to drive forward. But once again, the car refused to move.

A groan emanated from the back of his throat. He was stuck. He wasn't going to get his new car out of this mess without some help.

Tap-tap.

He glanced to the side to find the outline of a person holding a flashlight as they rapped on his driver's-side window. So he hadn't imagined the other car—a car that had been headed straight for him.

He rolled down the window.

"Are you all right?" a female voice called out over the noise of the wind and rain.

He squinted at her flashlight. She lowered the beam. "I'm okay. But my car needs help. Can you call for a tow?"

She straightened and checked her phone. "There's no cell service."

They were on their own on this dark stormy night. As though to confirm his thoughts, the whole sky lit up. A crack of thunder shook the ground.

Atlas's gaze moved to the crop of tall trees surrounding them. This was not a good place to be during an electrical storm. They needed out of there as quickly as possible.

There was another brilliant bolt of lightning followed by a crack of thunder. This storm was sitting right over them.

As though reading his thoughts, she said, "Come on. My car is over there."

He hesitated. "I can't just leave my car."

"Sure, you can. It's not going anywhere—at least not tonight. Are you a guest at the Ludus Resort?"

"Yes."

"Good. Let's go." She turned, and in her rush up the embankment she slipped in the mud. She landed on all fours.

"Are you all right?"

Before he could exit the car, she got to her feet and acknowledged that she was fine. By now she was soaked and muddy from her effort to help him.

With great reluctance, he grabbed his travel bags from the passenger seat and got out of the car. It was raining so hard that he was instantly soaked. As he carefully climbed the embankment, he could feel the rainwater seeping into his shoes. His back teeth ground together. Could this evening get any worse?

Once inside the car, he said, "You should learn to drive more carefully."

She hooked her seat belt. "What are you talking about?"

"You were driving in the middle of the road."

"I was not." Her restrained voice failed to mask her indignation. "Perhaps you were driving too fast for the road conditions—"

"I was not." Was he? He had been distracted. And perhaps he was taking his bad mood out on her.

He sat quietly while she slowly and carefully turned her car around. When she finally had the car straightened on the road, she barely pressed the accelerator. They were never going to reach the resort tonight if she didn't pick up the speed.

With a huff, he sat there stiffly. He stared straight ahead at the rain pounding the windshield. When they finally reached the resort, he'd insist they get someone out there to tow his car. He just hoped it wasn't damaged.

While she gripped the steering wheel with both hands, they rode on in silence. At last, the glow of lights hovered in the distance. Seconds later they came upon lampposts lining the road that led to the resort.

They parked beneath a fully lit portico. He glanced over at the woman as she undid her seat belt. Her long hair hung well past her shoulders. Even though it was wet, it had loose waves.

And when she glanced at him, he was immediately drawn in by her eyes, but she turned away before he was able to fully appreciate her beauty. She didn't say a word as she got out of the car.

He rushed to do the same. The large glass doors swept open, bidding them entrance to a marble floor that gleamed. In the center of the spacious lobby was a water fountain with lights that played off the droplets of water. It was surrounded by groups of light aqua upholstered chairs.

He glanced down at his wet clothes and shoes that were making a mess of the floor. He couldn't wait to go to his suite and get cleaned up. Except there was no one at the reception desk. He found a bell at the end of the counter. He banged his palm down on it, over and over again. He hoped the rest of the resort's service was better.

The woman covered his hand with her own. The touch jolted him from his thoughts. It felt as if an electric current had arced between them before racing up his arm and making his whole body tingle. His gaze met hers. It was then that he noticed the color of her eyes, brown with gold flecks. And right now, agitation radiated from them.

"Stop." She kept her voice low but firm.

He glanced down to where her hand rested on his. Her touch was warm and soft. As though realizing they were still touching, she swiftly moved her hand.

A door off to the side of the counter area opened. An older man rushed out. He struggled to place his black-rimmed glasses on his face. When his gaze collided with Atlas's glare, his eyes widened. And then the man took in Atlas's appearance. By the horrified expression of the desk clerk, he must look quite the mess. But it was his car he was worried about right now.

Before the clerk could utter a word, Atlas said, "There's been an accident."

The clerk's gaze moved from Atlas to the woman and then back again. "Is anyone hurt?"

"My new car. It's stuck out there in the mud. Someone has to remove it from the side of the road. And then I need to check in."

"Yes, sir. I can call for a tow and get you registered." The man hesitated as though not sure what to do first.

"Call them," Atlas said in his get-it-done-now voice.

That seemed to stir the man into action. A phone call later, the clerk wordlessly hung up. "No one answered."

"Surely there has to be someone working at this hour." He started to wonder how there could be a five-star resort in a place that was so far removed from a major city that they didn't have twenty-four-hour road service.

"I'm afraid not, sir. But I assure you it'll be a priority in the morning."

The morning? That wasn't good enough. The clerk had no idea how valuable his car was, but he would know soon.

Atlas opened his mouth to explain when the woman intervened. "That will be good, Titus. Perhaps we should get the gentleman checked in."

"Oh." Titus appeared startled out of a stupor of uncertainty. "Yes, I can do that." The man visibly swallowed. "Do you have a reservation?"

"I do."

The clerk typed something into the computer. "Last name?"

"Othonos."

"First name?"

"Atlas."

He waited, wondering if the man recognized the name. Moments passed. "There you are." The man's fingers moved rapidly over the keyboard. "You have one of our finest suites—the jungle suite."

"Sounds intriguing." Atlas glanced over to find the woman had moved toward the doors. Was she leaving? Atlas called out to her. "Surely you aren't thinking of going back out there."

"I need to go home."

"The ferry just left. It's the last trip tonight," Titus said.

The woman approached them. Her shoulders drooped. "What am I supposed to do now?"

"You could get a room for the night," Atlas suggested.

"That's not possible. The resort is fully booked." Titus sent the woman a hesitant look. "I'm sorry—"

"It's okay. I understand." A flicker of emotion reflected in her eyes, but she blinked it away before he was able to discern it.

Atlas told himself he should be happy that he'd inherited a profitable business, but he didn't think anything about his inheritance was going to make him happy—not until he signed the sales agreement. And that wasn't happening fast enough.

But in the meantime, he felt bad because if this woman hadn't stopped to help him—if she hadn't given him a ride to the resort—she would be on her way home. And now there wasn't even an available room for her to spend the night.

He turned his head, taking in the spacious lobby. There wasn't even a comfortable couch to stretch out on.

The last thing he needed was to feel bad because this woman had to sleep in her car. She'd done him a good deed, and so he'd do her one in return. "You can stay with me."

"I don't even know you."

He stepped up to her and extended his hand. "Hi. My name's Atlas Othonos. I'm the CEO of Atlas Securities. I can give you references. There's my assistant and—" He stopped himself from mentioning that his mother had owned this resort. It was a subject he wasn't prepared to delve into that night.

She eyed him up as though trying to make her mind up about him. "Thanks. But no thanks." She turned to the desk clerk. "Could you have a cot and linens sent to my office?"

Titus nodded. "Of course." And then the clerk turned to him. "If I could have your keys, sir, I'll see that your car is taken care of."

Atlas hesitated before handing over the car keys. "Thank you." He turned back to the woman. "You aren't planning to spend the night like that, are you?"

Her muddy clothes clung to her, and there were goosebumps lining her arms. Her face and lips were pale. A sense of responsibility passed over him.

She glanced down at her disheveled clothes. "I'll be fine."

As the air conditioner kicked in, she started to shiver and his concern grew. "No, you won't. Not like that. You need a hot shower and some dry clothes. If you won't stay in my suite, at least stay long enough to get a shower and warm up." A flicker of interest shone in her eyes. "Let's go."

Even though she was shivering, she shook her head.

"If this is about us being strangers, I'll wait here in the lobby while you use my shower."

Her eyes widened with surprise. "You'd really do that?"

"I would."

"But you're wet too."

"Not as wet or cold as you."

"There are actually two bedrooms in your suite, so you wouldn't have to wait your turn."

His thoughts suddenly took a steamy turn. "I hadn't planned to share my shower, but if you're offering—"

"I'm not!" Her cheeks took on a rosy hue. "That isn't what I meant."

The rumble of laughter started low in his chest and burst forth. His amusement resulted in her fine brows knitting together in a frown.

He subdued his amusement. "I'm sorry. It's been a really long day. If there are two bedrooms, it's all the more reason for you to warm up. I promise to be a perfect gentleman."

"I don't know."

"I'll just have a seat over here until you come back." He started toward one of the chairs in the lobby.

"Wait." When he turned back to her, she said, "You need a shower and dry clothes too. Let's go."

He thought of asking if she was sure but then thought better of it. He quietly let her lead the way. A hot shower would feel really good. The truth was he was exhausted and had absolutely no interest in sitting around the lobby. He'd been up extra early that morning to head to the airport. Maybe some sleep would make him less irritable.

"Here we are." The woman stopped next to an oversize wood door.

He opened it and gestured for her to go first. His gaze followed her into the room. She was unique, and he liked all things unique from cars to women.

CHAPTER TWO

TONIGHT HAD CERTAINLY taken an unusual turn.

Hermione stood in the suite not quite sure what to say to her undeniably handsome host. Maybe it was her being cold that had her tongue-tied. She rubbed her upper arms, hoping to chase away the chill that had taken hold of her.

Her gaze caressed his chiseled jawline before moving to linger on his kissable lips. Her attention swept up past his straight but prominent nose and came to rest on his light blue eyes framed with dark lashes and brows. He was drop-dead gorgeous. If he were a Greek god, she could imagine him being Zeus with his many lovers.

Why was a sexy man like him checking into the resort alone? It didn't happen often at the Ludus. Most often the resort hosted couples and families. It wasn't known as a singles spot.

Atlas ran his hand over his clean-shaven jaw. "Do I have something on my face?"

Heat flared in her cheeks. "Um, no. Sorry. You just remind me of someone."

"You already know who I am but I don't believe you introduced yourself." And then he sent her a dazzling smile that made her insides melt into a pool of desire.

"Hi. I… I'm Hermione Kappas." Good grief. Now he had her stuttering. And she realized she was once again staring at him. She quickly averted her gaze.

"It's nice to meet you." He held his hand out to her. She hesitated. What was it about him that had her feeling off-kilter?

She refused to let him know that his presence got to her. She placed her hand within his. His long, lean fingers engulfed her hand. His touch was warm, and it sent an electrical current up her arm that made her heart pitter-patter. As he gave her hand a gentle shake, she came to a conclusion—this man was dangerous to her common sense. She should get away from him as fast as her mud-covered heels would carry her. And yet her feet refused to cooperate.

He released her hand. "Thank you for the help tonight."

"Glad I was there to help."

Just then her stomach decided to rumble its complaint about its lack of nourishment. Lunch had been many hours ago. And she thought she'd be home by now.

"I…ah…should go get that shower." Her gaze

moved between the two bedroom doors. "Do you have a preference of which room you want?"

He shook his head. "Help yourself." As she started to walk away, he said, "Wait. You need some dry clothes."

He was right but she'd make do. She'd already imposed on him enough. But when she turned to tell him so, he was pulling clothes out of a bag.

"These will be big on you but at least they're dry." He tossed some drawstring shorts and a T-shirt at her.

She hesitated. The thought of warm, dry clothes was too much to resist. "Thank you."

She knew she should feel grateful for him going out of his way for her and leave it at that, but she had to question why he was trying so hard to be nice to her. Maybe it was just that she'd been on her own since she was seventeen when her mother had died. She'd learned the hard way that the only person you could count on was yourself.

The last man she'd trusted was her ex-boyfriend, Otis. Things had been good in the beginning. Then he'd moved in and she'd started to think they had a future together. What was the saying? Love makes you blind. That must have been what happened to her because in the end, she'd seen his true colors and she didn't like what she saw. That's when she'd kicked him out.

But she wasn't about to get involved with Mr. Tall and Sexy. However, it didn't mean she wasn't curious about the man. She wanted to know everything about him from where he came from to what he was doing on the island. And she was curious about one other thing… Her gaze strayed to his hands. No rings. Interesting.

He looked as though he wanted to say something more when his phone buzzed. "Sorry. I need to get this."

"No problem. I'm just going to go get that shower."

With his phone pressed to his ear, he moved toward his room. She turned and headed in the other direction.

She stepped inside her bedroom and closed the door behind her. Even though she'd previously been in this suite, it felt so different to be here as a semi-guest. She looked around, seeing her surroundings differently. She admired the beauty of the room and anticipated the luxurious comfort awaiting her. As a resort employee, staying in a guest suite was frowned upon.

But what did she have to worry about? It was only a shower and she was the boss…for now. Until the will was resolved, she could do as she pleased and there was no one to reprimand her. A smile pulled at her lips.

As she moved to the bathroom, she noticed that it was practically the size of her entire flat. No expense had been spared when this resort was built. And updates were completed on a regular basis.

She stepped farther into the room and admired the enormous white soaking tub. It beckoned to her. She really shouldn't give in. But she was already here, so why not indulge?

As she filled the deep white tub with warm sudsy water, she unwrapped a purple bath bomb and smiled as she dropped it in the tub.

She quickly undressed. An inspection of her stained and torn clothes had her placing them in the garbage. Then she stepped into the warm and inviting tub. As she soaked, her thoughts drifted to Atlas. She was quite certain he wasn't soaking in a tub, though that didn't stop her mind from conjuring up the very steamy image. Her heart beat faster. Oh, what an image!

His broad shoulders had hinted at a muscular physique. Not even his tailored suit could hide the fact that he worked out, probably daily. And boy did it pay off. Not that she was interested. Not even a little. Okay, maybe just a little.

But she had her career to think about now. And with the future of the Ludus up in the air, she had to be prepared to fight for the livelihoods of her employees. She just hoped it didn't come to that drastic measure.

CHAPTER THREE

SHE WAS UNFORGETTABLY BEAUTIFUL.

And an indulgence he couldn't afford right now.

Atlas wasn't at the Ludus Resort for a holiday. He was here to conduct business—at least that's the way he'd come to regard his mother's estate. Because to consider what it truly meant would mean scratching back scabs on old wounds. It would mean dragging to the surface emotions he'd worked for years to bury.

Now with room service ordered, he'd showered and changed into a fresh button-up and jeans. He rolled up his sleeves as he stepped out of his bedroom into the living room. He glanced around the suite, taking in the details from the palms and trees that soared up to the second-story ceiling with fake cockatoos and parakeets in the trees to the forest green wallpaper. He couldn't help but wonder how the other rooms were decorated. Or what Thea's private apartment was like—not that he wanted to spend time there. He wanted nothing to do with her things.

He turned his thought to his security business. For him, working was like breathing. His business was the reason he got out of bed in the morning.

Whereas people were unreliable, his business never let him down. It was there for him each day, and it rewarded him for all of his efforts. As it was, if he didn't work another day in his life, he would never want for a thing in his life.

But at this late hour, business was concluded in Europe. He grabbed his phone to check his messages and answered a couple of emails that he'd received while he'd been in transit to the island.

He decided to send a text message to his old friend, Krystof.

Have arrived. This resort has a lot of promise. Will send pictures soon.

He slipped the phone back in his pocket. No sooner had he done that than it vibrated. He withdrew it to find a response.

Looking forward to them. Can't wait to see in person.

Come now. We can see it together.

Can't. Playing cards in Monaco.

Krystof was always moving from one challenge or game of chance to the next. He was a nomad much like himself. But he was the one person Atlas knew and trusted that had the funds to buy this place.

Come as soon as possible.

I'll check my calendar. Maybe next week.

See you then.

Atlas returned the phone to his pocket. By next week, he planned to be finished with this part of his life. The sooner, the better.

He sat down on the hunter green leather couch, finding it surprisingly comfortable. In his vast experience of traveling from one place to another, he'd found most hotel furniture looked nice but ended up being terribly uncomfortable. Not so with the Ludus Resort.

Was it Thea who'd put all of the thought into this resort with its themed suites and furniture that not only looked good but felt good too? Not that he cared what Thea did. Just as she'd never cared what he did.

Knock-knock.

He welcomed the interruption. Thinking about Thea only angered him. Why she'd left this island to him seemed like some sort of cruel joke.

When he opened the door, he found a server wearing a black-and-white uniform pushing a white linen-covered cart with two covered dishes, and yellow and purple flowers in the center. Once the food was placed on the dining table next to the window overlooking the stormy evening, the cart was removed.

Atlas turned to find Hermione had emerged from her room. Her long hair was wet and hanging down her back. His clothes engulfed her petite frame. Even so, she looked adorable.

"Would you care to join me at the table?" He gestured to an empty chair.

She hesitated. "I don't want to intrude any further."

"You won't be. And I ordered enough for two. What do you say? Will you join me?"

She hesitated as though considering her options. "I did miss dinner."

"All the more reason for you to join me." He pulled out a chair for her before taking a seat himself.

She lifted the lid from her plate. "Breakfast food?"

He nodded. "I travel a lot, and I've found this food appetizing at any hour. I wasn't sure what you'd like, so it's a little bit of everything. But if you want something else, I'll call down to the kitchen. They are open twenty-four hours a day, but you already know that."

"This is fine. Thank you."

They ate quietly as though each were lost in their own thoughts—thoughts of the accident, thoughts of how their lives had collided and thoughts of what tomorrow would bring each of them. He turned his gaze to the window and stared out at the turbulent night as lightning etched against the dark sky.

If not for the storm, he would have missed meeting Hermione. She was different from the other women who'd passed through his life. Hermione wasn't chatty. She hadn't told him her whole life's story in the first five minutes of their meeting.

Instead, he found her to be a mystery of silent looks. Her eyes let him know there was a lot going on in her mind, but whatever her thoughts were, she was keeping them to herself. The quieter she became, the more he wanted to know what was going on behind her captivating brown eyes.

"Was your meal good?" he asked.

She nodded. "It was."

And then she looked at him like she was trying to read his thoughts. She wasn't the first one to look at him that way. But he liked to think of himself as unreadable.

"Will anyone be joining you?" she asked.

He couldn't help but wonder where this conversation was headed. He thought of his invitation for Krystof to join him here on the island, but he knew that wasn't what she meant. But she didn't appear to be trying to hit on him. So what was her angle?

Curiosity got the best of him. "No."

"No wife? Or girlfriend?"

She surprised him with her very pointed questions. "Just me."

It wasn't that he didn't have relationships—if that's what you wanted to call them—it's that he wasn't any good at them. At least that's what he'd been told as the women exited his life.

Maybe he didn't try hard enough to make any of the relationships work. Or maybe they saw what his mother had seen in him—he wasn't worthy of love. Either way, he focused all of his energy on his business. It hadn't let him down.

Hermione nodded as though he was giving all of the right answers. "This just doesn't seem like the sort of destination for a single man."

He sat up straighter. "Why not?"

She shrugged. "The resort doesn't exactly have much of a nightlife or an abundance of single women."

His gaze moved to her hands. No rings. He ignored the excitement that raced through his blood. He hadn't intended to have a holiday fling, but now he was reconsidering his options.

"What about you?" If she could ask personal questions, so could he. "Are you single?"

She hesitated. "I am."

He smiled. "See. I didn't even have to look around and yet I found the most beautiful single woman on the island."

That's all it took to bring a rosy hue to her cheeks. And it made her even more attractive. Oh, yes, a holiday fling was becoming more appealing by the moment.

"You probably say that to all of the women." She reached for her water glass and took a sip.

"Trust me. I don't throw around compliments lightly." It was true. He used them sparingly and only when he truly meant them.

As his phone vibrated in his pocket, it reminded him that he had his hands full while he was on the island. He had to stay on top of his security business while cleaning out Thea's apartment and retrieving all of the documents in her personal safe. In addition, he had to make sure the property was ready to hit the market. And he planned to have it all done in less than two weeks.

In order to meet his aggressive timetable, he had to stay focused on his mission. But maybe Hermione could help him in a different way. "How much do you know about the island? I mean you must know most everything, right?"

She shrugged. "What are you curious about?"

"This is my first visit here." *And my last.* "As

you probably know, this resort doesn't have a website. And there really aren't many pictures of it online."

"That's because the island has a privacy policy. It gives the rich and famous a chance to unwind and enjoy themselves without the risk of ending up in a tabloid."

"But doesn't it make it hard to lure in new visitors?"

"Not really." She frowned at him. "You make it sound like you're a journalist." And then her eyes narrowed in on him. "Listen, if you're here to write some exposé—"

"I'm not a journalist." When she continued to stare at him with suspicion reflected in her eyes, he said, "I swear. I'm not."

"You sure sound like one."

How was he supposed to convince her that he wasn't a journalist? "Do you really think a journalist could afford to stay here?"

She paused as though giving the idea consideration. "Your publisher could pick up the tab."

He inwardly groaned. She wasn't going to give him any slack. And then he had an idea. "Wait here." He moved to his room and quickly returned. He sat down and handed her a card. "This is my business card."

She read it. "You install security systems like they sell on television?"

He couldn't help but laugh at her underwhelmed

expression. It'd been a long time since someone didn't recognize him or his company. "Not exactly. Atlas Securities develops and installs very sophisticated systems."

She yawned. "I'm sorry."

He found himself smiling at her bored expression. She was definitely unique. The more he got to know her, the more he liked her. "It's okay. My business doesn't excite everyone."

"No, it's not that. It's just been a really long day. I had to finish a special project and it wiped me out."

"What sort of project?"

She shook her head. "You don't want to hear about that tonight or I'll put us both to sleep." She yawned again. "We should call it a night."

"Agreed." He set aside his napkin and got to his feet. "Are you sure I can't convince you to stay in the guest room?"

She shook her head and then walked away. At the door, she turned back. "Thank you for the shower and food." And then color bloomed in her cheeks. "And the clothes."

When she started out the door, he asked, "Will I see you again?"

"It's a big resort. Probably not." And then she was gone.

He was sorry to see their evening end so soon. They were beginning to be friends and he liked that idea. Having a friend on the island might make his job here less painful. Maybe tomorrow he'd seek her out—to help him find his way around the island. Yes, that sounded like a fine idea.

CHAPTER FOUR

HAD LAST NIGHT been some sort of dream?

When Hermione opened her eyes the next morning, she glanced around, finding herself in her office, wearing clothes that most definitely weren't her own. Last night had been no dream.

She wasn't ready to move. Not yet. She closed her eyes, and her mind filled with the image of the handsome man she'd met last night. At first he'd been rather testy, but then he'd offered her a hot bath, food and the clothes off his back. Okay, maybe they weren't off his back, but it had been a kind gesture. She lifted the T-shirt to her nose and inhaled the faint spicy scent that clung to the soft material. Mmm… She inhaled again, deeper this time.

The alarm on her phone went off. She reached for it on the floor and checked the time. As her gaze focused on the numbers, she groaned. She needed to get moving.

The first thing she did was call one of the resort's boutiques and request they send over an outfit. Next she located some sample toiletries in her bottom desk drawer. She took them to the ladies' room where she styled her hair into her usual French twist. She liked its sleek professional look and the way it kept her long hair out of her way as she leaned over her desk to review reports.

After rushing through her morning routine, she returned to the office and called the car garage about Atlas's…er… Mr. Othonos's vehicle. They promised to immediately see to towing and detailing it.

Knock-knock.

She swung open the office door to find a young woman with a rack of clothes. Hermione didn't recognize her. Her gaze moved to the name tag: Iona. She must be one of the new hires. Now wasn't exactly the right moment for an introduction.

She quickly sorted through the selections. The clothes that had been chosen for her were of bright, cheerful colors, everything Hermione wasn't feeling right now. She picked the least vibrant shade, a peachy-pink-colored outfit. She thanked the young woman and sent the rest of the clothes back to the boutique.

Her gaze moved to the price tag on the outfit. She stifled a moan. The clothes cost as much as her monthly rent, but what choice did she have? Her navy-blue business suit had been stained, and there had been a tear across the knee from when she'd fallen. She'd left it in the trash back at Atlas's suite.

When she was ready to face the world—ready to face Atlas—she headed for the door. She moved quickly through the quiet hallways. The closer she got to Atlas's suite, the faster her pulse raced. Last night, she told herself she wasn't going to see him again, but…well…she did have his clothes. And she really should thank him again for all he'd done for her last night.

When she stopped in front of his door, her palms grew clammy. Before she lost her nerve, she knocked.

When Atlas opened the door, his gaze met hers. She felt as though she could drown in his mesmerizing blue eyes. Her heart thump-thumped in her chest. And when he smiled, she noticed how his eyes twinkled. She subdued a dreamy sigh.

She forced herself to look away. If she didn't get the words out quickly, she feared she'd forget her reason for being at his door.

"Here are your clothes." She handed them to him. "Thank you for last night—"

Someone cleared their throat.

Oh, no! He isn't alone.

She glanced past him and into the room. Hermione's heart sunk down to the white canvas shoes she'd been supplied by the boutique. There before her stood Adara Galanis, the resort's concierge and her friend. When their gazes met, Adara's eyes momentarily widened in surprise.

Atlas stepped back and bid her entrance to the suite. Hermione didn't know what to say as she stepped forward. Heat engulfed her cheeks as he closed the door behind her. How was she supposed to explain any of this?

Atlas cleared his throat. "This is Hermione. She came to my rescue last night and ended up stranded on the island."

Adara's startled gaze moved between her and Atlas. "I heard about the accident and as the concierge, I wanted to personally offer my services. If there's anything I can do—"

"Yes, you can make sure my car is detailed and inspected," Atlas said.

"I've already taken care of your car," Hermione said. "It was the first thing I did this morning."

Adara sent her a concerned look. "Hermione, are you okay?"

"Perfectly fine. Not a scratch on me." She tried to sound calm and in control, but being this close to Atlas made her insides shiver with nervous energy. "His car was the only one involved in the accident."

His gaze moved between the two women. "You two know each other?"

"Of course," Adara said. "Hermione is the resort manager. She didn't tell you?"

His gaze narrowed on Hermione. "No. She failed to mention it last night."

At first she'd kept her position from him because he'd been agitated about his car. And later it was just easier to keep things casual. The muscles around Hermione's chest tightened like a vise.

"I can explain," she said.

Atlas shook his head. "I don't have time for explanations. I'm expecting a very important business call." He turned to walk away. "Just go."

"Wait. Give me a moment to explain." Hermione moved to block his exit.

His gaze caught hers. The anger reflected in his eyes stopped her in her tracks. He walked around her and strode into his room. The door closed behind him with a resounding thud.

The breath trapped in her lungs. She had totally messed this up.

First, there had been the downpour followed by his accident. And now she'd made a huge miscalculation by not admitting last night that she ran the entire resort. A little voice in her head said to just walk away. It didn't matter if he liked her or not. They would never see each other again. But there was this other part of her that had started to like him.

Resort manager.

He was still surprised to learn Hermione was in charge of the resort. He couldn't help but notice how she'd purposely left out that detail last night. He couldn't help but wonder why.

Had she recognized him? Had his mother shown her a press release of him? Surely not. Thea's life hadn't had room for him.

The questions mounted one right after the other. He raked his fingers through his hair as he tried to discern what sort of angle Hermione was working. Usually he was able to see a con from afar but with her, he hadn't sensed a thing.

Whatever. He had work to do—contracts to review, emails to answer and that phone call that still hadn't come. All in all, he didn't have time to play games. In his spacious bedroom, he sat down at the large desk facing the wall of windows overlooking the beach, but he didn't take the time to appreciate the beauty of the scenery. Instead, he opened his laptop and set to work.

As his fingers moved over the keyboard, his thoughts repeatedly drifted back to Hermione. He replayed their meeting in his mind. Perhaps he hadn't made the best first impression. He wasn't usually this agitated.

Perhaps Hermione hadn't announced her position because he hadn't made her feel comfortable enough to reveal her true identity. And there was the fact that he hadn't admitted who he was either.

Knock-knock.

When he didn't immediately respond, Hermione called out, "Mr. Othonos, can we speak?"

He pressed Send on an email to his assistant in the London office. "I'll be out."

Her heels clicked over the marble floor as she retreated. He didn't rush out to speak to her. He wasn't used to being summoned. He was the one who did the summoning. And so he answered one more email.

Then he quietly joined her in the living room. He glanced around, finding that they were now alone. As though she sensed his presence, she turned. Their gazes met and held for a second too long. In that moment, he forgot about his irritation with her.

Her dark hair was pulled back in a much too severe style. He imagined unpinning her hair and letting it flow down over her shoulders. Definitely better. His fingers tingled with the temptation to comb through her long silky locks.

And then there was her beautiful face with dimples in her cheeks. High cheekbones led to a pert little nose, but it was her brown eyes that drew him in. His pulse spiked. And when a smile pulled ever so slightly at her lips, he realized that he'd let himself get distracted for much too long.

He glanced just past her left shoulder and out the window at the gray sky. He cleared his throat. And then proving to himself that he had control over his reaction to her nearness, his gaze met hers again. "Why weren't you honest about who you were last night?"

Emotions flickered in her eyes, but in a blink, they were hidden behind a wall of diplomacy. "I'm sorry if you feel I was in some way dishonest with you."

Her restrained manner and resistance to admit her error only succeeded in further agitating him. "I didn't ask for an apology. I want an explanation."

"You were dealing with enough last night with your car going off the road—by the way it will be delivered a little later this morning."

"I hope they're careful." He frowned at her. "You know none of this would be necessary if you had stayed on your side of the road last night?"

She opened her mouth to argue with him but wordlessly closed it. In the light of day, she couldn't deny that she forced him off the road.

He expected to feel some sort of satisfaction at her acknowledgment of fault, but he didn't. Okay, it wasn't exactly an acknowledgment. It was more like a lack of denial. Either way, he'd been in the right and her in the wrong.

She blinked and then two lines formed between her fine brows. "I can assure you the garage does exceptional work."

"You don't understand. That car is unique. There's not another one out there like it." When she still looked confused, he said, "It's a kit car with every upgrade you can imagine. I just picked it up. I'm planning to have it shipped back to London."

She looked at him like he'd just spoken a foreign language. She obviously wasn't a sports car aficionado. "I thought you would be happy to have it back as quickly as possible."

He raked his fingers through his hair. She was right. He wasn't usually this on edge. It was being here in this place—Thea's place. He didn't want to be here.

"Of course," he said. "Thank you for seeing to it. This place just unnerves me."

The words had crossed his lips before he'd realized that he'd said too much. His pulse raced. It was though the earth had shifted beneath his feet. A moment ago he'd been Atlas Othonos, founder and CEO of Atlas Securities, and soon he would be known on the island as Thea's son. It was a title he hadn't worn since he was a little boy. It was a title he never thought he'd have again.

Hermione's gaze searched his. "I don't understand."

"Thea is, er, was my mother."

Her eyes widened. "We heard the island had been inherited, but we weren't even sure Thea's son was still alive."

"Why wouldn't I be alive?" His voice came out harsher than he'd intended.

Had his mother told everyone he was dead? The thought sickened him. It was one thing not to want to be a part of his life but quite another to want him dead. Could his mother have been that cruel?

"I'm sorry," Hermione said. "It's just none of us have ever seen you around the resort."

How did he explain this? And then he decided he didn't have to explain any of it. It was none of her business.

"My mother and I weren't close." That was as much as he was willing to admit. It wasn't anything Hermione couldn't surmise on her own. "But I would appreciate if you kept this information to yourself."

"You don't want anyone to know that you now own the resort?" Hermione asked.

"No, I don't. At least not yet."

"But you'll want to get to know the staff right away—"

"No, I won't."

Her diplomatic expression slid from her face. In its place was a look of surprise. "Why not?" Her eyes widened as though she realized she'd just vocalized her thoughts. "I mean is there a better time for you to tour the resort?"

"I don't need to see it. I'm selling it." He pressed his lips together.

He hadn't intended to tell anyone about his plans yet, but there was something about Hermione that had him acting out of character. Now he braced himself for a barrage of reasons that selling the resort was a bad idea.

"What? But why?" Her gaze searched his.

"I can't keep it." Still she sent him an expectant stare so he added, "My life isn't here. It's in London." It wasn't the whole truth but it was enough of it.

Concern reflected in her eyes. "But what about the resort? Will it be kept the same?"

Once again he raked his fingers through his hair. She wanted answers from him that he didn't have. "I don't know. That will be up to the new owners."

"But you haven't even seen the resort yet. You might change your mind about selling it."

He shook his head. "The sale is going to happen. The only question is when. Now if you don't mind, I have work to do."

He walked her to the door. He could tell the wheels of her mind were turning. This conversation might be over for the moment, but he had no doubt she would broach the subject in the near future. And his answer would be the same—the resort was for sale.

CHAPTER FIVE

THIS MORNING WAS not going well.

That was one of the biggest understatements of her life.

Hermione wondered what else could go wrong. Her steps were quick as she hurried down the spacious hallway. She forced a smile to her face as she greeted everyone she passed. It wasn't her staff's fault that she'd had the most unfortunate run-in with the resort's heir. Or the fact that he was the most stubborn, annoying man to ever walk the earth. Okay, maybe that was a bit over the top, but he really got under her skin.

How could Atlas not even slow down and consider keeping the island? Who wouldn't want their very own island? Wasn't that what dreams were made of?

But, no. He didn't even want to hear about how profitable the resort was, or how it basically ran itself, so his immediate intervention wasn't needed…or wanted.

Now what was she supposed to do? Start looking for a new position elsewhere? The thought left a sour feeling in the pit of her stomach.

The Ludus Resort was more than her place of employment. It was her makeshift home. Without having any relatives of her own, she'd adopted the resort employees or rather they'd adopted her. She wasn't quite sure of which way it'd happened. But the point was she would be lost without this great big, loving group of people.

She glanced at her smartwatch. She had almost two thousand steps already. It was the pacing she'd done in Atlas's suite. And now it was five minutes before the start of the workday. She'd meant to get to her office much sooner, but the run-in with Atlas had taken longer than she'd anticipated. Not that her pleading had done a thing to sway his decision about the fate of the resort.

Her assistant, Rhea, glanced up from her desk as Hermione walked through the doorway. "Good morning."

So far there was nothing good about it. Still, it wasn't Rhea's fault. Hermione forced another smile to her lips. "Morning."

Rhea's gaze followed her as she crossed the outer office to her doorway, but her assistant didn't say another word.

With the door closed, Hermione's thoughts returned to Atlas. She'd always wondered what had happened between Thea and her son. Her friend was always light on the details of their estrangement, but Hermione was starting to figure things out. And she didn't like what she saw.

In fact, she was really worried. She sank down on her desk chair. Whereas the Ludus was steeped in traditions from the employees' monthly luncheon to the annual regatta, Atlas didn't seem to care for tradition.

She blew out a frustrated sigh. More changes were coming to the Ludus. And she would predict that they weren't going to be good for her or the staff. Even worse, she didn't know how to stop Atlas. How did you stop an heir from doing what they wanted with their inheritance?

"Hermione?" Rhea's voice interrupted her troubling thoughts.

She glanced up. "What did you say?"

Rhea hesitantly stepped in her office. "I asked if everything is all right."

"Uh, yeah. Perfect." Everything was so not perfect. It was anything but perfect.

"That outfit is pretty. Is it new?"

Hermione glanced down and wanted to say that it was just something she'd pulled out of the back of her closet, but she couldn't bring herself to lie. It just wasn't who she was. Instead, she nodded.

Rhea smiled. "I was tempted to buy it."

She was so busted. "I… I just decided to splurge."

Rhea's eyes sparkled with amusement. "What's his name?"

"What?" Heat immediately rushed to her cheeks. "It's not like that. There is no he. Surely you don't think I had a one-nighter with a guest." She pressed her lips together to keep from rattling on and digging a hole deeper for herself.

"It's okay. Relax. I heard about the accident."

"You did?"

She smiled and nodded. "Titus let me know you had a rough night."

The heat in her cheeks increased until the roots of her hair felt as though they might instantaneously ignite. "It's not like you're thinking."

"I'm thinking that you got stranded on the island and there weren't any available rooms so you slept in your office."

"Oh." Hermione was caught off guard. It took her frenzied mind a moment to catch up with reality. "It is exactly what you were thinking."

Rhea stepped out to her desk and soon returned with a pair of scissors in hand. She approached Hermione. "Stand up and turn around."

"What?" She really needed some caffeine because she was having problems following Rhea's words. "Why?"

She continued to smile at her. "Trust me."

And so Hermione did as she was told. There was a distinct snip and then Rhea adjusted the neckline on Hermione's top.

"Okay. You can turn around."

When she did Rhea was standing there holding a tag. Oops. She'd been in such a rush that morning that she'd forgotten to remove it. She inwardly groaned. She wondered how many people had seen the tags hanging off her clothes.

Atlas! He would have seen her blunder. The heat rushed back to her cheeks. The best thing she could do was just keep her distance from him. It was obvious she didn't think clearly around him and in turn she rubbed him the wrong way.

"Thank you."

"Anytime. You would have done the same for me."

Hermione nodded. Friends watched out for each other. "Now I'm going to go hide in my office all morning. If anyone wants me, I'm not here."

Rhea arched a brow. "Seriously?"

Hermione sighed. "No. But it is tempting."

Rhea closed the door on her way out, giving Hermione a chance to gather herself. Perhaps she took more comfort in her morning routine than she'd realized because she felt utterly rattled and out of sorts.

She moved to her coffee maker and brewed a cup. She was never more grateful than now that it only took a couple of minutes to create a steaming cup of coffee. She added some sweetener and creamer and gave it a stir before carrying it to her desk.

It was there that she settled into her work, and

soon she was caught up in reviewing department budgets and approving large disbursements. For a moment, she forgot about everything, including the man with the sky-blue eyes.

She didn't know how much time had passed when there was a knock at the door. She glanced up to find Adara standing there. "Do you have moment?"

Hermione waved her in. "What's up?"

"I just wanted to tell you how sorry I am about this morning. I didn't mean to make things awkward for you."

If she was upset with anyone, it was herself. "Don't worry about it. And just for the record, I didn't spend the night with him." She explained how she'd used the shower and then slept in the office. "Thank goodness I didn't. He's Thea's son."

Adara's eyes widened as her mouth gaped. "He is?"

She nodded. "It came out after you left. He was upset that I hadn't told him I was the manager."

Adara settled on the arm of the chair across from Hermione's desk. "Why didn't you?"

"Because he was really upset last night, and I didn't want to make things worse."

"And how are things with you two now?"

Hermione leaned back in her chair. "Not good. He's selling the resort."

Her eyes widened. "He is?"

She nodded. "I offered to give him a tour but he declined. He said he had work to do."

"So he's in his suite working instead of enjoying all of the resort's amenities?"

"I guess so. I haven't checked on him."

"Don't you think you should? I mean if he sells this place, everything is going to change. You need to show him that he's making a big mistake."

Hermione shook her head. "You didn't hear him. He's very determined. And he's angry with me because he thinks I ran his precious car off the road last night."

"Oh, no. That's not good. Did you apologize?"

"No." Her response came out harsher than she'd intended. "I didn't do anything wrong. The road was flooded. He must have overcorrected and gone off the road. Anyway, I had the garage tow his car today. They're cleaning it up and having it delivered this morning."

Adara nodded. "So then he had nothing to be upset about. You should try again and show him that the Ludus is special."

Hermione resisted the urge to roll her eyes. "I don't think anything will convince him of that. Certainly not me saying it. It's like he arrived on the island all set to hate the place and anyone associated with it."

"Then give him things to like about the Ludus—like the employees." Adara smiled brightly. "We're a great group, if I do say so myself. Once he meets us, he'll have to like us."

At last Hermione smiled. "You think that highly of this group?"

"I do. I really do." Adara pondered the idea for a moment. "You know the best way to immerse him in the atmosphere is to bring him to lunch today."

"Today?" She shook her head. "I don't think he'd be interested in a covered dish lunch. He doesn't strike me as the social type."

"We'll see about that." Adara stood. "You get him to the lunchroom and I'll spread the word that we need to melt his frosty exterior. After all, he's Thea's son. Surely he has a heart in there somewhere." She made a quick exit.

"I wouldn't count it," Hermione muttered under her breath.

The last thing she wanted was to deal with that man again. He was like a grumpy old man. Only he wasn't old; in fact, he didn't appear to be much older than her. And maybe he did have a reason to be grumpy. After all, if she'd just picked up a new car, she'd probably be upset if it went off the road and got stuck in mud.

And then there was the death of his mother. Close or not, that had to hit him hard. At the very least, it had to make him feel his mortality. It was one of the many things she'd felt when she lost her own mother.

She sighed. Had she really just talked herself into giving him another chance? It would appear so. She just wondered how he felt about home cooking because that's what they served for their monthly employee luncheon.

His phone rang nonstop all morning.

Atlas frowned as he stared blindly at his laptop. The voice of his vice president sounded over Atlas's speakerphone. He knew he shouldn't have come to the island. He'd only been gone one night and there were already problems. He should be back in London so he could go to the office and straighten out this mess in person.

But on a good note, by midmorning a resort employee had returned his keys. His car was now safely tucked away in the resort's private garage. Atlas had immediately given it a thorough personal inspection as well as a short test drive. Thankfully no damage had been done.

"What do you want to do?" The VP's voice drew Atlas from his meandering thoughts.

He gave his company's problem some serious thought. "I want the head of our installation department to fly to the embassy, and I want him to do what needs to be done to fix this problem. And I want him on a plane today."

"Yes, sir. I'll see to it."

"Make sure you do. Because as of now, this is your highest priority. No. This is your only priority. The embassy is counting on us to get this right or we can forget about any future national security contracts."

"I'm on it."

"On second thought, I want you on the plane too. I need someone on the ground who can smooth things out." He'd do it himself, but that would mean dragging out the mess with Thea's estate even longer.

There was a distinct pause on the other end of the line. "Yes, sir."

"Keep me updated."

Ding-dong.

"What was that, sir?"

"That is an interruption I don't need right now. See that this problem is corrected." And then Atlas ended the call.

Ding-dong.

Someone was certainly impatient. He couldn't imagine who it might be. He swung the door open and was surprised to find Hermione had returned so quickly. For a second, his voice failed him. Had they set up a meeting and he'd forgotten about it? No. Not possible.

"Can I help you?" he asked.

She sent him another tentative smile that didn't go all the way to her eyes. Then as a happy couple strolled by, Hermione waited until they'd moved further down the hallway before speaking. "Can we talk?"

He opened the door farther and stepped aside. "Come in." After she'd stepped inside, he said, "I don't have much time. You'll have to make it quick."

"Have you been in this suite all morning?"

"Yes. I have work to do."

"So why come to the island?" She looked at him expectantly.

His body stiffened. So much for them starting over. "You know why I'm here, to deal with my mother's things."

"You could have just had someone box up her things and ship them to you."

She was right. Why hadn't he done that? Why hadn't the thought even crossed his mind? When he'd received news of her death via his office, his first thought was to come here. But by the time he'd heard the news, the funeral was over. He was left figuring out why he suddenly felt so much more alone on this great big planet.

His brain said he shouldn't feel anything about Thea's passing. After all, it wasn't like they were a part of each other's lives. And that had all been her decision. She's the one who walked away and left him behind.

And yet there was this hollow spot in his chest that felt as though something was now missing. He refused to explore that feeling further. He was here to do a job, nothing more.

He cleared his throat. "Is there a reason you're here, Ms. Kappas?"

"It's Hermione. And yes, there is a reason. Have you eaten lunch yet?"

Was it that late, already? He consulted his Rolex. Yes, it was that late. "No, I haven't."

"Then come with me." She started for the door without even waiting for his response.

He started after her, prepared to set her straight. "Listen, I don't have time to go to lunch with you." He was out the door, trying to catch up with her. "I have work to do."

She paused in the hallway to glance back at him. "And you have to eat in order to do your work." She gestured behind him. "Don't forget to close the door."

He glanced over his shoulder to find she had him so distracted that he had walked out the door without a thought to closing it. He retraced his steps and did just that. Then he took long, rapid steps to catch up to her.

"I don't think you understand," he said. "I run a huge international security company. I have things that need my attention." Just then his stomach growled as though in protest to him trying to skip out on another meal.

She glanced over at him and arched a brow. "You need to take care of you. And besides, I think you'll enjoy this lunch."

He sighed. "Couldn't we just order room service?"

She shook her head. "This is better than room service. Trust me."

That was the problem. He didn't trust her. He didn't even know her. Still, he walked with her. Maybe he'd order some food to take back to his room.

They appeared to be heading away from the lobby and common areas, which he found odd. Why wouldn't the restaurants be in highly trafficked areas? Perhaps it was something the new owner should correct.

Hermione swiped her employee card to open a set of heavy steel doors. He caught the placard on the door that said: No Entrance. Employees Only.

"Where are we going?" He glanced around the brightly lit hallway, taking in the buzz of voices mingled with the hum of machines.

"You'll soon see. We're almost there."

Maybe he had been a little too focused on his work, but that was how he'd built his company to be one of the biggest and best in the world. The only problem with being the biggest and best was that there was nowhere to go from there. It was though his drive was starting to wane and he found himself looking for a new challenge. He just didn't know what that would be. Nor did he have time to figure it out—not with the embassy problem to sort out.

Just as he was about to tell Hermione that he didn't have time for this expedition, she stopped in front of a door. She turned to him with a smile. "We're here."

Here? He glanced around. This wasn't a restaurant.

Hermione opened the door and stepped inside. He followed her because he'd come this far, he might as well see what this was all about.

The first thing he noticed were the delicious aromas. They smacked him in the face and sent him spiraling back in time to when he was a little boy. He recalled how much his mother used to love to cook. Their kitchen used to be filled with the most delicious aromas of fresh herbs, clove and allspice. He hadn't thought of that in a long time.

Another memory came flooding back of his mother saving him leftovers from his favorite meals. She would say growing boys needed extra helpings. His father didn't agree. And so she would hide the food and let Atlas eat it when his father was at work. He'd felt so special, so loved—

He gave himself a mental shake, pushing away the unwanted memory. Because the only thing that mattered was that Thea had left him.

His gaze scanned the room as he tried to figure out why they were here. The room was filled with tables and people—lots of people. Most were dressed in work uniforms from maid outfits to cooking staff and some in janitorial coveralls.

Atlas stopped and turned to Hermione, feeling as though he'd somehow been set up. "What are we doing here?"

"I thought you'd want to meet the employees. They are excited to meet you." And without giving him a chance to say that it was the last thing he wanted to do, she turned to the people. A hush had come over the crowd as they stared at him as though trying to decide what to make of him. "Hi, everyone. I'd like you to meet Thea's son, Atlas. He is the new owner of the resort and I hope you'll give him a big, warm welcome."

Suddenly people surged forward with their hands outstretched. Some wore smiles while others sent him hesitant looks. They all wanted one thing from him—the knowledge that their lives weren't about to change. This was exactly what he'd been hoping to avoid. They wanted a promise he couldn't give them. And so he artfully darted around the subject of the future of the resort. Instead, he found himself focusing on the here and now—which meant promising them that he would tour the resort.

It felt as though he'd just fallen into a trap—a trap set by the beautiful manager. He'd most definitely underestimated her. He glanced around for Hermione, but she'd disappeared into the sea of Ludus employees.

It would appear this was some sort of special employee luncheon. He missed the part about why they were holding such a luncheon, but he was handed a plate. Food was heaped on it, so much so that it took both of his hands to hold it.

Now he felt obligated to view the resort because one thing he wasn't was a liar. And he had Hermione to thank for this latest development. So if he could miss work to tour the grounds, so could she. Although the thought of spending more time with the crafty manager didn't sound so bad; in fact she intrigued him.

It was working.

Or perhaps it was a bit of wishful thinking.

Hermione couldn't decide if Atlas was putting on a good show for the employees or if he was starting to let down his guard with them. She hadn't spoken to him throughout lunch. It wasn't that she was avoiding him, it was that he was constantly surrounded by employees greeting him.

But now that lunch was over, the crowd was thinning. Atlas approached her. It was impossible to tell what effect the luncheon had on him. His poker face gave nothing away.

He leaned in close to her ear. "That little trick wasn't very nice of you."

"Would you have agreed to come if I'd have told you we were eating with the employees?"

"No. Because it won't change my mind about the sale."

She resisted the urge to sigh. She'd never met such a stubborn man. Maybe Adara could reason with him because she was done with him. "Well, I need to get back to my office—"

"Not so fast. Thanks to your plotting, I've now promised the employees that I'd tour the resort and I've chosen you to be my guide."

"Me." This had to be a joke. He didn't even like her.

The corners of his mouth lifted in a devious smile. "Where shall we start?"

Her phone buzzed, distracting her. She withdrew her phone from her pocket and checked the screen. "Something has come up. I must go."

"Not so fast. If I'm going to miss work for this tour, so are you."

She shook her head. "You don't understand. The royal jewels have arrived. I must go sign for them."

"What are royal jewels doing at the resort?"

"I don't have time to explain now. Do you remember how to get back to your suite?"

"I can manage. But I'm coming with you."

So all it took were some famous jewels to spark his interest in the resort. If she'd have known, she'd have mentioned their pending arrival for the upcoming Valentine's Day Ball much sooner.

The holiday was not quite two weeks away. She couldn't help but wonder if Atlas would be attending.

Perhaps there was more to this resort than he'd originally thought.

There was definitely more to its general manager than he'd first suspected.

She wasn't above pulling out all of the stops if she felt something was important, not only to herself but to those around her. He respected her determination, but it wasn't enough to change his mind. Nothing would convince him to keep this island.

Still, he was curious to learn why royal jewels had been delivered to the resort. It could possibly be a selling point. He was quite certain most resorts didn't play host to royal gems. Perhaps he'd been too quick to dismiss the idea of touring the resort.

His security expertise might come in handy. He liked the thought of doing some manual labor instead of answering the unending list of emails awaiting his attention. And it would give him a chance to know the general manager a little better—from a business standpoint of course.

"Do you really expect me to believe these jewels are royal?" It had to be some sort of PR campaign to draw in more guests.

As they made their way along the hallway, she glanced at him. "You really don't know much about your mother, do you?"

He'd made a point not to know anything about her. If Thea could so easily forget him, he could forget her. "What is that supposed to mean?"

Hermione shook her head. "The jewels are real, and they are from the royal family of Rydiania."

He vaguely recalled hearing of the country, but he couldn't place where he'd heard the name. "Why would they send the resort jewels?"

"The prince visits every year."

So they'd worked out some sort of arrangement with this prince. Interesting. "I want to know why this prince would agree to such an arrangement."

Hermione stopped walking and turned to him. She waited for a family to pass, and then she lowered her voice. "Which part would that be—the part where the prince is your step cousin? Or the part where your mother married a former king?"

He didn't recall his mouth opening but it must have happened, because a little bit later when his mind came out if its stupor, he pressed his lips together. This couldn't be right. Thea had married royalty? No. Really? None of this was making sense to him.

Hermione continued walking. "Your stepfather, Georgios, had already abdicated the throne by the time he'd met your mother. In fact, they met right here on this island. She was a maid and he was a lonely, sad man, who missed his family as they'd disowned him. In that way, Georgios and your mother felt as though they had something in common—"

"I didn't disown my mother. If that's what she told you, it was a lie." His words were quick and sharp.

"No. I'm sorry. That isn't what I meant. I shouldn't be telling you any of this. It isn't my story to tell."

He sighed in frustration. "It's me who should be sorry. I didn't mean to snap. This is just a lot to take in."

Sympathy reflected in her eyes. "I can't even imagine what you're going through. When my mother died, our circumstances were different. We were very close. I'd been able to say goodbye."

"I'm sorry for your loss."

She resumed walking. "Thank you. It was quite a while ago. Although there are times when something happens and she's the first one I want to tell. And then the loss comes washing back over me. We were as close as a teenager can be to their mother."

"I didn't know my mother when I was a teenager. She took off when I was five. And my father and I were anything but close." It wasn't until he'd spoken the words that he realized he'd never admitted any of this before. But there was just something about Hermione that made it easy for him to open up. Perhaps too easy.

It was best to focus on business. He didn't want to dredge up any more memories of himself at five years old, crying into his pillow for his mother—a mother that would never come back for him—at least not for many years.

He cleared his throat, hoping when he spoke his voice didn't betray the raw emotions raging within him. "Having the jewels here, it's quite a liability for the resort to take on, perhaps too much. What if something were to happen to these royal jewels? It'd put the resort in quite a difficult position."

She stopped walking and turned to him. "It's what your mother wanted."

He opened his mouth and then closed it. He had a sinking feeling this wasn't the first or the last time Thea's memory or wishes would be an issue. "But she's not here now and I am."

Hermione's eyes narrowed. "What are you saying?"

He wasn't going to delve back into the subject of his relationship with Thea. The fact was this island and the resort were now his responsibility. And until it was sold, he had to do what he thought was best for the business.

He met her gaze straight on. "I'm saying that I'm not comfortable with this arrangement with a prince I've never heard of."

"And yet you're the one that didn't want to get too involved with the resort or its employees, remember?" Her eyes glinted with agitation. "This resort is my responsibility—at least until the resort is sold."

He didn't want to make an enemy of her. He'd already heard the employees sing her praises. They would go to battle for her. And all of that would hamper any hope of a sale.

He needed to divert this conversation. "We should get moving. They'll be waiting for you."

She gave him an intense stare. "I know you have your reasons not to like this place, but I love it and its people. You would too if you let down your guard. Regardless, I will fight to maintain our ways."

"Change is inevitable, whether it's coming from me or someone else. Now let's not be late."

She was nothing if not observant. He'd prefer if she didn't read so much in him. It made him feel exposed and vulnerable. It was a position he wasn't used to being in. And one he hoped not to be in again.

CHAPTER SIX

SHE DIDN'T THINK she could do it.

There weren't many things that defeated her, but Atlas's stubborn disposition about retaining ownership of the resort might be one of those things.

Hermione grew quiet as they approached the large glass doors of the Ludus Gallery. She was still processing the fact that the rift between Atlas and his mother went so much deeper than she'd ever imagined. While her heart went out to him, she still had an obligation to her employees. No matter what, she couldn't give up on changing his mind about keeping the resort.

Perhaps he needed to remember the good parts of his relationship with Thea. Were there good parts? She thought of Thea—kind, generous and caring Thea—yes, there had to be good parts. Maybe he'd forgotten them. Maybe he didn't want to remember them. But Hermione knew that until her dying day, Thea had loved her son.

Something awful had gone wrong. Hermione

couldn't fathom what it might have been. Atlas might try and tell himself that it didn't matter after all of this time, but it did matter to him. If it didn't matter, he wouldn't be here.

She wanted to help him find some peace. She told herself that she would be doing it in memory of her dear friend, who had given her a hand up when she'd needed it most. It was her chance to pay back Thea's kindness.

She stopped next to the thick frosted glass doors before she reached for the oversize brass handle. Atlas grasped it. He opened the door for her. She thanked him as she stepped inside the gallery.

"This part is currently open to the resort guests," she explained. "But if you'll follow me to the back area, it's where we're preparing for the Valentine's Day reveal."

There were a few people here and there, admiring the latest watercolor acquisitions. Hermione glanced over at the six-piece collection of seascapes. Though they were all of the same scene, each displayed a different time of day, from a morning scene to an evening sunset. Each was so detailed that she could stand there for an hour or two and still not catch all of the minute details.

"Do you do these special exhibitions on a regular basis?" Atlas's voice drew her from her thoughts.

"While the resort owns the pieces on display out here, the ones in back are the ones on loan from other museums or countries." She stopped and turned to him, hiding her excitement that he was finally showing some interest in the resort. "We try to always have something special either on display in the back room or in the planning stage."

She used a key to open the door to the sealed-off section. She held the door for Atlas. He was intently inspecting the door, which she found surprising when there was so much else to see back here.

"Is everything all right?" she asked.

"I was just surprised that there isn't higher security for this section."

"We haven't had any problems with it so far."

"That's what everyone says before they're robbed."

She frowned at him. In a low voice she asked, "Are you saying we're going to be robbed?"

"No. I was just thinking that your security needs to be upgraded."

She glanced around, hoping they weren't overheard. "Perhaps you should think about those matters a little quieter."

"We can discuss my ideas for the new system later."

She didn't speak for a moment, not trusting what would come out of her mouth. "I don't think that's necessary. This system was just installed last year."

"And as you pointed out, this is now my resort."

She wondered when he would play that card. "The jewels are this way. I can't wait to see the Ruby Heart. I've seen pictures, but that is never the same as seeing it in person."

She didn't think of herself as the jewelry type. There was only one piece of jewelry that she cared about—her mother's locket. But it was lost to her forever. Still, there was just something exciting about viewing jewels that have been worn by queens and princesses.

An armed guard stood in front of the room where the Ruby Heart was to be displayed. He nodded at them.

"Is it in the display case yet?" she asked.

"They're waiting for you before they unpack it."

"Understood." She started past him.

The guard stepped in front of Atlas, impeding his entrance. "You can't go in there. Only approved employees."

"I'm with Hermione."

"There are no exceptions."

"Are you serious?" Atlas's voice grew deep with agitation.

"Absolutely."

"It's okay," Hermione said. "He owns the resort."

"It doesn't matter if he's the president. If he hasn't had a full background check and been added to my list, he can't go inside."

Her gaze moved to Atlas. "I'm sorry. We can get this straightened out later. The security firm doesn't work for the resort."

"It's okay. Do what you need to do. I'll be fine here."

She wasn't so sure he would be fine. He looked more like a caged animal as he started to pace. But people were waiting for her, so she moved into the secure room. While the rest of the gallery had white walls to make it feel airy and spacious, this section was done with black walls and ceiling.

Spotlights were used to highlight the specific items on display. Nothing was to distract from the features of the show. And it worked. It drew people's gazes where they needed to go. But the spotlights hadn't been set up yet as the star of the show had just now arrived.

A couple of royal guards stood with the locked box. She knew the procedure. She had to produce two forms of identification and have her fingerprints scanned. Then she signed the digital receipt. Once all of that was complete, one of the guards entered the security code that released the digital lock.

The Ruby Heart was revealed in all of its sparkling grandeur, and Hermione was left speechless. She didn't know a gem could look that impressive. She felt bad that Atlas wasn't able to see it. But if he stayed until Valentine's Day, he could see it once it was secure in its display case.

"Did I miss anything?" Atlas's voice came from behind her.

Hermione spun around. "What are you doing back here? How did you get past the guard?"

He held up his phone. "Remember, I own a security company. I have connections around the world. I called up the owner of this security firm, and I was immediately added to the list."

"You were?" She blinked. "But it normally takes weeks for the background checks."

"I have top security clearance in a number of places, including Greece. I have to for my work." He moved closer and stared at the gem. "So this is the beauty that's causing all of the problems?"

"Isn't it beautiful?" She was still in awe over it.

"It's not bad."

"Not bad? Are you serious? It's one of the biggest rubies in the world."

"I'm just giving you a hard time. I think it is quite impressive."

"And look, there's a brass plaque with it." She moved closer to read it aloud. "'The legend of the Ruby Heart. If destined lovers gaze upon the Ruby Heart at the same time, their lives will be forever entwined.'"

Heat warmed her cheeks. She suddenly regretted reading the legend. Not that they were lovers—far from it.

"Whatever works," he said.

"What does that mean?"

"It's clearly a gimmick. A lure to draw in an audience." His gaze moved to her. "Surely you don't believe it, do you?"

Did she believe the legend? Of course not. Did she want to believe it? Maybe. Was it so wrong to believe in eternal love?

"No." She wasn't about to tell him how she truly felt. After signing for the other royal jewels, she turned to Atlas. "We should get moving and let these men take care of things."

"Now that I know there are priceless gems on the grounds, I'm definitely having my people upgrade the security. You can never be too safe."

"That won't be necessary."

"Sure, it is."

She pressed her hands to her hips. "Are you saying the current security isn't good enough?"

"I'm saying it could be better."

What she heard was that the security system that she'd painstakingly researched and ultimately chosen wasn't any good. Was he right? Had she made a costly mistake?

She stopped herself. He was doing the same thing to her that Otis used to do—make her doubt herself. The current security was more than sufficient.

She opened her mouth to tell him that, but then she realized this might be a way for Atlas to invest himself in the resort. And though it took swallowing a bit of her pride, she chose to put the future of the Ludus first. "It sounds like you have a plan. Let me know what you'll need from me."

"I will." He grabbed his phone and started texting someone.

She could only imagine he was contacting his office. For a man anxious to keep his distance from this resort, he was getting more involved by the minute. But she resisted pointing this out to him. She didn't want to scare him off. In fact, she was looking forward to him staying around much longer.

This place could definitely use his expertise.

The next day, Atlas had gone over the resort's blueprints and made arrangements to fly in his best crew. A resort this size was going to take a lot of work, but it was doable. And then when the place was sold, it would be a selling point. In his book that was a win-win.

But he'd gotten so caught up in the security aspect of the resort that he still hadn't toured the place. And the tour would let him scope out the best type of security for the different areas.

At least that's what he told himself when he went to track down Hermione and collect on the tour she still owed him.

He had just opened his suite door when he spotted her walking down the hallway. "Do you have a moment?"

"Sure." She followed him into the suite. "What do you need?"

"I believe you owe me a tour of the resort. After all, we wouldn't want me to lie to the employees, right?"

She opened her mouth as though to disagree with him, but then she wordlessly pressed her lips together. He noticed her pink shimmery lip gloss and her lush lips. They were so tempting. So very tempting. He wondered what it'd be like to kiss her. Would one kiss be enough? And then realizing where his thoughts had strayed, he raised his gaze.

He couldn't help but wonder if she knew what he was thinking. He hoped not because it wasn't like him to let pleasure get in the way of business. And right now, this was his most important business. Because the sooner he wrapped things up here, the sooner he could leave the past in the past.

"I don't have a lot of time. Where do you want to start?" she asked.

"Wherever you choose will be fine."

She reached for her phone. "Let me update my assistant."

He knew showing him around was the last thing she wanted to do. But then again, she'd been the one to get them into this situation. He checked his phone while he waited for her. Just then a message popped up from Krystof.

We need to talk.

Agreed. If you don't want the island I need to find another buyer ASAP.

Commence your search for another buyer.

That wasn't the news he wanted to hear. A sale to Krystof would be fast and painless. But trying to line up another buyer wouldn't be so simple.

You still planning to visit?

I'm not sure.

A frown pulled at Atlas's mouth as he slipped the phone back in his pocket. He moved to the floor-to-ceiling windows. Now that the rain had moved on, he noticed the lush green foliage. So this was after all a beautiful sunny Mediterranean island. Buyers would fight to own it. Wouldn't they? There might even be a bidding war. Or was he being overly optimistic?

"Sorry about that." Hermione slipped her phone back in her purse. "Shall we go?"

They entered the spacious hallway with plush red carpeting that silenced people's footsteps. Hermione led the way. She hadn't stated their destination and he hadn't thought to ask. All the while, he was taking in his surroundings from the expensive and notable artwork on the walls to the crystal chandeliers.

"Are all of the rooms normally booked?" He hated the fact that he knew so very little about this property. He had a lot to learn and quickly.

"Yes. The reservations fill in well in advance."

"Really?" His voice came out quite loudly in the quiet hallway.

"This is an exclusive resort that offers privacy and pampering. Our clients return regularly."

"It can't be that great."

Hermione arched a fine brow. "You'll soon see."

A couple of employees passed by them. They smiled and silently nodded in greeting. This appeared to be the time of the day when the resort was abuzz with employee activity as suites were cleaned.

An older woman pushed her cleaning supply cart toward them with a big, friendly smile on her face. When she reached them, she paused. "Hermione, I'm so sorry I missed the luncheon. We're shorthanded this week so I picked up a few extra rooms. You know, if everyone pitches in it makes it easier for everyone."

"Thank you, Irene," Hermione said. "Your efforts are greatly appreciated."

Irene turned her attention to Atlas. The smile slipped from her face as she stared at him. He wanted to ask what she was doing, but he already knew—she was looking to see if he had any resemblance to his mother. He didn't.

"You must be Thea's son." As his back teeth ground together, she continued, "We're happy to have you here. My condolences on the unexpected passing of your mother. She was the kindest woman. You were lucky to have her for a mother. I always thought she died from a broken heart. I just wanted to say how sorry I am for your loss. I'll let you two get on with things. I have another room to clean."

The woman's well-meaning words tore at his scarred heart. The Thea these people knew was not the same person he had known. He knew he should thank the lady, but the words bunched up in the back of his throat.

As they continued walking, Hermione asked, "Are you okay?"

He nodded. No, he wasn't, but he refused to let on to Hermione.

He swallowed the lump in his throat. "The people are friendly here."

"Yes, they are. It's a really great place to visit and work."

"If the resort is so great, why haven't I heard of it?"

"We have no need for the media…" Her voice trailed off as though she were lost in thought. "We have a mailing list that goes out regularly to our select clientele. And from there our guests use word of mouth to spread the news to other visitors."

It was inconceivable to him that in this day and age a resort could be amazing enough to generate sufficient business by guests returning regularly and recommending it to their family and friends. After all, it was just a giant hotel. Right?

Okay, so maybe the suites were on the lavish side, but there was no way they could do that for the rest of the resort. After all, there had to be limitations. No place was that incredible. He didn't believe it.

He glanced at Hermione as they walked through the resort. "How long have you worked here?"

"Since I was eighteen. In some ways, I feel as though I grew up here."

He noticed that she didn't feel the need to elaborate. He wondered in what ways, but he didn't ask. If she were to confide in him, she would expect him to do the same in return. And he'd already said more than he'd intended.

Atlas rubbed the back of his neck as memories of his youth came rushing back to him. They hadn't had much money growing up. Whatever they had his father spent on expanding his auto business.

Atlas hadn't always enjoyed his current state of creature comforts, including a small fleet of unique sports cars. He knew what it was like to do without. His father had withheld money as a way of controlling him. It was only when Atlas had finished university and went into business for himself that he became wealthy. But it never stopped him from getting his hands dirty if the need arose.

If he were to keep the island, he would change things. He would make the island less exclusive and open to everyone. It wouldn't be as lavish as it was now, but it would still be a fun destination. But it wasn't like he was entertaining thoughts of keeping the island. No way. He wanted the sale to go through as quickly as possible.

"Are you staying for the Valentine's party next weekend?"

"I don't think so." The idea most definitely didn't appeal to him. He didn't do hearts, flowers and romance. "Even if I am still here, I won't be attending."

"You won't want to miss it. The party will be spectacular."

"I'll be too busy." He averted his gaze.

He hadn't planned to share any of this with Hermione, but he was quickly finding it was very easy to talk to her. He'd have to be cautious around her or he'd be opening up about all of his secrets. And he didn't want to do that.

CHAPTER SEVEN

SHE WAS DOING FINE...

If fine included the imminent possibility of losing her job.

But it was the resort employees that Hermione worried about the most. Some of them had worked at the Ludus longer than she'd been alive—talk about devotion to their occupation.

She knew what it was to get bounced around in life and having to reinvent herself time after time. Even though she'd grown quite comfortable working here, she could reinvent herself again as a hotel manager or something else, but she didn't want to do it.

She chanced a glance at the heir to the Ludus Resort. As her gaze touched upon his handsome face, her heart raced. He was busy taking in his surroundings, giving her a chance to study him. He wasn't smiling. There was a firm set to his jaw. What was he thinking? Was he calculating the resort's monetary value?

It was as though the happiness had been sucked

out of Atlas. She felt bad for him, which most people would find odd since he was the one who was about to upend her life. What had happened to him?

Buzz-buzz.

She lifted her phone to find an urgent message from Nestor, the resort's event coordinator. It was regarding the special effects for the Valentine's party. "I'm afraid the tour will have to wait. There are some urgent disbursements that require my signature."

"Perhaps I could come with you." His gaze met hers, sending her heart rate into triple digits.

She wanted to tell him no. She needed some space so her pulse could slow to a steady pace. But when she opened her mouth, she said, "It won't take long."

"Even better."

She messaged Nestor that she'd meet him at her office. And so they set off for the administrative suite. Hers was the largest office, as well as having the prime spot in the corner. When she passed by her PA's desk with Atlas hot on her heels, Rhea arched her dark brows as unspoken questions reflected in her eyes.

Hermione paused and made introductions.

Rhea was her usual sweet and charming self. And to Hermione's surprise Atlas soaked up Rhea's pleasantries and returned them. It was though he'd transformed into another person on the way here. Because if that wasn't the case, it meant he didn't enjoy her company. The last thought nagged at her.

After a minute or two, Hermione moved into her office. She wasn't sure if Atlas was going to follow her or stay in the outer office chatting with Rhea. But then he joined her and closed the door behind him. He made himself comfortable on a chair facing her desk while she took a seat behind the desk. As she logged onto the computer system, she found herself glancing over the top of her monitor and noticing that he'd retrieved his phone and appeared to be scrolling through messages.

She got to work, but she kept finding her attention drawn to Atlas. When he'd glance up and catch her staring, heat would flood her cheeks.

Knock-knock.

"Come in." Hermione pressed Send on an email.

Nestor stepped into the office. His tan face lit up with a warm smile. She noticed how he was starting to take on some gray at his temples even though he was in his early forties with a young family.

She introduced Atlas and the men shook hands.

"How's the party coming?" she asked.

Nestor's face lit up. "It's on track to be our biggest and best. I think the guests will be impressed."

That was the kind of news she liked to hear. "What would we do without you?"

He continued to smile. "Hopefully you'll never have to find out."

Hermione resisted giving Atlas a sideways glance. "Do you have the disbursements and backup?"

He nodded and handed them over.

These were sizable payments. She tied in each number, initialed where required and then signed the bottom of the requisition.

After Nestor left, she continued to work. A half hour later Hermione was finally done. She pushed her chair back and stood. "I'm all set to go."

Atlas glanced up from staring at his phone with a confused look on his face as though he'd been totally lost in his thoughts and had no idea what she was talking about. "Sorry. What?"

"I didn't mean to interrupt you." She wondered what had him so preoccupied.

"No problem." He got to his feet and opened the door to the outer office.

"Do you still want to tour the resort?"

His dark brows furrowed together. "Why wouldn't I?"

"It just seems like you have something else on your mind."

"My mind is on seeing the resort. I have a promise to keep."

She had a feeling there was something he

wasn't telling her. Well, she knew there was a lot he wasn't telling her, seeing how they were virtually strangers. A niggle of worry ate at her.

Thea had once encouraged Hermione to follow her dreams wherever they would lead her. In fact, she'd pushed for Hermione to finish her higher education and even paid for it. She owed Thea a huge debt of gratitude.

Thea had been so nice. She would speak with all of the staff just like they were family. She'd inquire about the staff's children, grandchildren and pets. Thea was very down-to-earth, so much like her husband.

But Atlas was nothing like his mother. Where Thea was open and welcoming, Atlas was closed off and distant. Where Thea had a fair complexion and was short in stature, Atlas was dark and tall. The only glimmer of Thea that she could spot in Atlas were his eyes. He had his mother's sky-blue eyes.

"Where are we going?" His voice drew her back to the present.

"I thought we would start with a visit to the spa."

"The spa? Do I look like the spa type?"

"Honestly, I don't know what type you are as I just met you last night, but you wanted to see the resort and the spa is a huge part of the resort. It's near the lobby."

"That seems like an odd place for a spa."

"Why? It's not like people wonder around in their robes. Trust me, the spa is a world unto its own." She walked a little farther in silence and then came to a stop in front of two large wooden doors with oversize brass handles. "Here we are."

He remained quiet as they stepped inside. The young woman behind the desk practically drooled at the sight of Atlas. The woman's obvious infatuation with him aggravated Hermione. She told herself it was the woman's obvious lack of professionalism that bothered her and nothing else. She would have a discreet word with the woman's supervisor later.

After Hermione had stated the purpose of their visit, the young woman said, "I'll send someone out to give you a tour."

Once the woman walked away, Atlas turned to Hermione. "I thought that's what you were going to do."

She shook her head. "I can't."

"Why not?" His tone carried a note of displeasure.

"Because I... I'm not that familiar with the spa." The surprise that flashed in his eyes made her feel embarrassed.

Did he think she wasn't good at her job because she didn't know the intimate routine of the spa? Because she was very good at her job. She had department heads and supervisors that saw to the little details. And when there was a problem they couldn't resolve, she stepped in.

Suddenly she felt as though she didn't measure up in Atlas's eyes, and that bothered her. She'd worked very hard in her life to get this far. She was proud of how she'd gone from having nothing after her mother died to being able to put a roof over her head and now she was in charge of one of the world's most glamorous resorts. But she supposed none of that would impress Atlas. Wait. Did she want to impress him?

Part of her screamed out that yes, she did. But she quickly silenced that little voice. She didn't need his approval or any other thing, except her job.

"But you work here," he said.

"As the general manager." Why was he making a big deal of this? She lowered her voice. "Staff doesn't make use of the spa. It's reserved for guests only."

He frowned at her response. "That's a silly rule."

At that moment, a young woman in bright aqua scrubs approached them. "Mr. Othonos?"

"Yes." Atlas turned to the woman.

"We're ready for you."

"Good. Right now, we—" he gestured to himself and Hermione "—are going to have massages."

"I can wait here," Hermione said softly.

"Nonsense. You are my guest. I insist."

"You mean you won't get a massage unless I do?" She'd never faced such a predicament.

A smile spread across his handsome face. "That's exactly what I mean."

Adara's words echoed in her mind about making him comfortable here. But a spa treatment? Really? And during work hours? This was totally unheard-of.

"If it makes you feel better, as owner of the resort, I'm giving you the afternoon off and free access to the spa." His gaze dared her to challenge him.

It didn't make her feel better. She hated how he picked when he wanted to play the owner card. If he wanted to be involved in the resort's policies and management, he needed to fully commit himself. Otherwise, he needed to leave things to her.

Both Atlas and the attendant looked at her expectantly. She knew to back out now would cause even more tension with Atlas. Maybe it was best to indulge him this once.

"Fine. But I don't have long."

He sent her a satisfied grin. He seemed to like challenges and especially winning them. She tucked that bit of information away. She might need it in the future.

And so they took a tour of the sprawling two-story spa followed by chocolate massages. Hermione opted for a hand massage with a mani-pedi with *Kiss Me Pink* polish. Atlas agreed to a full-body massage. She could only hope it left him in a much better disposition.

Things needed to change.

Atlas didn't like the resort's atmosphere of haves and the have-nots. It reminded him too much of his childhood. His father had it all, and he had to beg for what little he got.

His father was big about the haves and have-nots. His father, being a small business owner, believed he was part of the "haves." He'd preached to Atlas that if he wanted to be someone in this world, he had to be rich like him—rich being a relative term. Back then his father made Atlas beg for new clothes or shoes when the old ones no longer fit.

These days Atlas tried not to waste his time thinking about his father—a father who said Atlas would never amount to anything just like his worthless mother. Atlas wondered what his father would think if he knew how much Atlas was worth now. He could buy his father's auto dealership many times over. And the fact that his mother had gone on to own and run this impressive resort would really get to his father.

But money hadn't changed Atlas. He hadn't become rich because of his father; he'd become successful in spite of his father. All he'd ever wanted to do was help people. And that's how he'd gotten started in the security business. He wanted to give people a sense of security—something he never had growing up. A state-of-the-art security system wasn't quite the same as the safety of a loving family, but it was as close as he could get.

And then he reminded himself that it wasn't his job to approve or disapprove of things at the resort. That particular responsibility would belong to the new owner. He just didn't know who that would be at this point.

He hadn't given up hope on changing Krystof's mind. But this was too important not to seek out other potential buyers.

As they passed by a poster advertising the grand Valentine's Day Ball, Atlas started to get an idea. He pulled out his phone and texted his real estate agent.

I want to invite potential buyers to a party at the Ludus Resort.

People like parties. When?

Valentine's Day. But there's a problem.

What sort of problem?

The resort is booked solid. Guests would have to stay on the mainland.

Not good. Let me think about it. Talk soon.

He slipped his phone back into his pocket. He was pretty proud of himself for coming up with a potential way for buyers to see the resort at its finest and with the royal jewels on display.

But his next thought was that if they worked out the logistics, he'd be obligated to attend the Valentine's ball. It was the sort of scene he worked hard to avoid. But if he focused on business, perhaps it wouldn't be so bad.

His gaze moved to Hermione. She would be at the ball. Suddenly he imagined her in a glittering dress with her long hair down around her slender shoulders. He imagined taking her in his arms and holding her close. The image was so tempting. Maybe a main course of business with a side of pleasure wouldn't be so bad after all. He didn't allow himself to think of what dessert might be.

"What did you think?" Hermione's voice drew him from his thoughts.

Having lost track of their conversation, he asked, "Think about what?"

Hermione's brows scrunched together. "The spa."

"Oh. It was nice."

"If you would like, I can arrange for you to spend more time there."

He shook his head. "I'm afraid the rest of the

tour will have to wait for another time. It's getting late, and I have some urgent calls to return."

"I understand. I, too, have work awaiting me. I'll see you tomorrow."

"Yes."

And then she was gone. Suddenly he felt very alone. It was as though she were all bright and sunny and now with her gone, a long, dark shadow had fallen over him.

Which was utterly ridiculous because he was used to being on his own. It'd been that way since he was a child. He didn't need someone in his life—someone to share his time. His business was all he needed.

He used to be able to sell that line to himself, but lately it wasn't ringing as true. For a second, he thought of going after Hermione and asking her to have an early dinner with him.

Buzz-buzz.

He glanced at his phone. It was a call from the embassy where he'd sent his men to resolve a problem with their system. With a sigh, he took the call and started walking in the opposite direction from Hermione.

CHAPTER EIGHT

HE WAS GETTING DISTRACTED.

And that wasn't good.

Thursday morning, Atlas had set up his temporary office in his suite. The problem at the embassy was more elusive than originally imagined. He'd done his best to help troubleshoot from afar. It was very frustrating not to be there.

That's why his very next phone call had been to his real estate agent. The sooner the resort was sold, the sooner he could get back to his life.

"So far there hasn't been a lot of interest in the island, but it's still early in the search," the agent said. "The lack of publicity has buyers hesitant."

"But the place is booked solid."

"That's definitely a selling point, but when it comes down to your island resort, well, it's remote and doesn't have a reputation with world travelers. The big hotel chains are going to go with a known location over something that isn't easy to reach. And I have to be honest with you. A lot of the properties are changing hands right now, so your resort is going to have competition."

He raked his fingers through his hair. "So what you're saying is that you can't sell the resort?"

"No. What I'm saying is that we need to build a portfolio, starting with the resort's history. I did an internet search but couldn't find much. Do you know the history?"

"Uh, some of it." He thought about his mother's marriage to a former king. But he wasn't ready to share that information. "I'll find out more."

"Good. And I'll arrange for one of our best photographers to come out and take photos. The images will be used for prospective buyers as well as growing a social media presence. Does this place even have a website?"

He hesitated. She wasn't going to like his answer. "No."

She clucked her tongue. "That's not good. I'll hire a designer and be in touch."

"When will the photographer arrive?" He didn't want to drag out his stay.

"I'd have to check on his schedule, but I'd say in a week or two—"

"Two weeks?" He once again raked his fingers through his hair as he stood and started to pace.

"I could try and find someone with an earlier opening on their calendar, but I couldn't vouch for their talent."

They couldn't be that bad, right? "Good. Do that."

He promised to forward her the required information. After he disconnected the call, he couldn't concentrate on business matters. He was frustrated that getting rid of his mother's island and resort was proving to be so difficult.

He needed to see Hermione. Maybe the resort had a professional photographer who could speed things up. At least that was the excuse he told himself when he went in search of her.

When he arrived at her office, her PA informed him that Hermione was dealing with a problem in the resort's gallery. He didn't have to request directions; he recalled how to get there.

He made his way across the resort. When he found Hermione, she was in the back of the gallery signing paperwork.

"Another delivery?" he asked.

Her gaze lifted to meet his. "As a matter of fact, yes." She gestured to the large canvas behind her. "It's called *Clash of Hearts*."

He gazed at the artwork with its hot pink and silver hearts entangled together. The conjoined hearts were repeated in varying sizes all over the canvas. "It's different."

She smiled. "You're not a modern-art fan?"

He shrugged. "Art is okay."

"So it's the hearts you have a problem with?"

This was not a subject he wanted to delve into. He cleared his throat. "I need your assistance."

"I'm sorry. I really don't have time. We're a bit shorthanded right now."

"Is that why you're here signing for a painting?"

"Yes. The woman who oversees the gallery went out on maternity leave." Hermione pulled out her phone. "I'll message Adara. She can help you with whatever you need."

"No. It has to be you."

She drew in a deep breath as though subduing her frustration. "Why me?"

"Because you knew my mother."

Her brows drew together. "Yes, I did. We were good friends." She hesitated. "What do you need help with?"

"A couple of things. First, does the resort have a professional photographer on retainer?"

She shook her head. "We've never needed or wanted one."

Of course they didn't. That would have made things easier for him.

The silence dragged on before he spoke again. This was something he'd given a lot of thought. "I want to know if you'd assist me on going through Thea's things."

"Oh." She was quiet as she absorbed this information.

"I need the help and with you being her friend,

I thought you might know what she'd want done with her things." Not giving her a chance to back out, he said, "What can I do to convince you to help me? Name your price." That was how badly he didn't want to face his mother's things alone.

This was his fourth day on the island, and he hadn't even stepped foot in Thea's apartment much less started sorting her items. He knew if he didn't get help that he'd keep making excuses to avoid it.

He could see the wheels in Hermione's mind turning. She was going to turn him down, and he couldn't really blame her. This wasn't her mess to clean up. And she'd already taken time out of her busy schedule to make sure he enjoyed his stay.

"If I help—" her voice drew his full attention "—will you make sure the resort's staff is retained by the new owner for at least six months?"

And there she went again, impressing him with her generosity. Most people would have asked for something for themselves, but Hermione thought of others instead of herself.

"Done." He was unable to deny such a selfless request, even though it would hamper any sale negotiations.

"And the employees won't lose the seniority and benefits they've so rightly earned." Her voice was firm.

"Done and done. Anything else?"

She shook her head. "If you help them out, I

will help you, but it will have to be in the evenings. I still have a day job."

He held his hand out to her. "It's a deal."

She looked at his hand before her gaze rose to meet his. And then she placed her hand in his and gave it a firm shake. For an instant, he considered tightening his grip and drawing her to him. He had this growing urge to kiss her—to feel her lush lips pressed to his. He wondered how she'd react.

As he continued to stare into her eyes, he felt his heart pound. What was it about this woman that had such an effect over him?

And then he realized he was making too much of things. After all, he was already out of sorts with being here on his mother's island with the dread of having to go through her personal items hanging over him. As well as learning how happy she'd been here—without him.

It was a lot to deal with at once. It was no wonder his mind was so quick to find a diversion. And that's what this infatuation with Hermione was—a break from reality. He withdrew his hand, already missing the softness of her touch.

His mouth grew dry. He swallowed hard. "Why don't we continue the tour of the resort?"

She frowned at him. "Right now?"

"Is there a problem?"

She hesitated as though she were thinking up an excuse to get out of it. "No. Of course not. Let's go."

And off they went on a walking tour of the resort, from the play area for the children and those who were young at heart with their ballroom and art room to the casino, which looked as though it belonged in Monte Carlo with its gold, flashy slot machines and table games to the gold-trimmed ornate ceiling and enormous crystal chandeliers. The staff was all dressed up in pressed white dress shirts, wine-colored vests, gold neckties and black pants.

Atlas started to get an idea. "Would there happen to be a high rollers room?"

Hermione arched a brow. "You like to play cards?"

"No. I'm not asking for myself."

She led him outside the casino. They walked a little way and then turned a corner. There stood one of the largest bouncers he'd ever seen. The man was taller than Atlas as well as wider.

Hermione stopped at the end of the hallway. "The private room is there. I believe there's a poker game in progress. You'll need to wait until it ends to go in."

"That won't be necessary." This might be just what he needed to lure Krystof to the island. "What's the buy-in?"

"It's high."

"How high?"

"A hundred."

"Thousand?" When she nodded, he said, "Interesting."

"Would you like a seat at the table?"

"No. I don't gamble on games of chance, but I do know someone who would be very interested."

They continued walking until they came to the indoor pool area that had not one or two but four long slides with skylights overhead. The area was filled with smiling people and rambunctious children. He had to admit that the resort did a fine job of offering entertainment for most everyone.

Next to the pool area was a food court with cuisine from around the world. They decided to have a late lunch there. Hermione opted for fish tacos while he chose a gyro with lettuce and tomato topped with *tzatziki* sauce and a side of *sfougata* cheese balls.

"What do you think of the resort?" Hermione asked after finishing her two tacos.

"I think it's like a small city with a lot to offer the guests."

"And you haven't even seen the outside."

"I still can't believe Thea owned all of this." There was a part of him that wanted to know more about her. "Was she happy here?"

"Very much so. She loved her husband dearly, and this island was her whole world."

He shouldn't have asked. He didn't want to hear about Thea's perfect life—a life that didn't include him. What was it about him that made her reject him? Was he that unlovable?

"I don't understand why Thea left this place to me." He was still asking himself why she'd done it.

"I'm not. She never stopped loving you."

He wanted to believe Hermione, but his mother's actions or rather her lack of action where he was concerned told him all he needed to know about his mother's feelings toward him. There was something inherently wrong with him that his own mother rejected him.

"My mother and I had a lot of unresolved issues."

"Is that why it took you so long to come to the island?"

"I was away in the States when I was notified of Thea's passing." As he said the words there was a twinge of pain, but he refused to acknowledge it. "I should have dropped what I was doing to deal with the solicitors but…"

"But what?"

He was about to brush off her inquiry when his gaze met hers and he saw the genuine concern reflected in her eyes. "But my mother and I hadn't been close since I was a little kid. I… I didn't, well, I didn't realize what all was involved with her will."

"You didn't know that she owned an island much less a hugely profitable resort?"

"I had absolutely no idea about any of this. When I knew her, my mother didn't have much—certainly not when she walked away from my father." Atlas rested his elbows on the table and gazed at Hermione. "But you knew someone different."

She smiled, but it didn't quite reach her eyes. She missed his mother; that much was obvious. "We all knew and liked her. Thea was very involved in the resort."

His back teeth ground together. Thea had been very involved with what mattered to her—the resort—not him. He'd already been dismissed by not just his mother but his father as well. His father was all about his auto business and stroking his own ego. If you didn't look up to his father and regard him highly, he didn't have time for you—even if you were his own flesh and blood.

Atlas preferred to be on his own because then no one could hurt him. It also gave him the ability to come and go as he pleased, never staying in one place for too long. Never getting too attached to anything or anyone.

"Atlas, what is it?" The concerned tone of Hermione's voice drew him from his thoughts.

He shook his head. "Nothing."

"You know you can talk to me. I'm an okay listener."

He couldn't help but smile. "Just okay?"

She smiled and shrugged. "A great listener

sounds like bragging, and if I said I was a terrible listener you wouldn't say a word. So I went with the middle of the road description."

He laughed at her explanation. Hermione was exactly what he needed right now. She was like a ray of sunshine on a cloudy day. And what they were about to do was going to be so hard. Thankfully Hermione would be there to hopefully take the edge off the painful task.

Hermione nodded. "What would you like to see next? I can take you to our indoor golf driving range or our tennis courts."

He shook his head. "As tempting as that sounds, I have something else in mind."

"What would that be?"

"I... I'd like to see my mother's apartment."

"Certainly. Let's go."

Hermione quietly led the way from the food court. All the while he took in the decor of the building. A lot of it was old, but it was all elegant and well cared for. It was like being in an older home that had been loved and preserved through the years.

Atlas couldn't help but think that there was still room for updates. He was certain the buyer would want to do a total remodel to bring the place up-to-date with the rest of their global properties. Of course that would mean the resort would lose some of its unique charm, but there were always trade-offs to keep things modern. It's what he told clients when his team had to make adjustments to properties for their security equipment.

Speaking of security equipment, not only the gallery but the entire resort could use a complete overhaul. He was a bit surprised they hadn't hired his company in the first place. They were the best in the business. Or did his mother purposely not hire him? It was another prick to his heart.

After stopping by her office to pick up the key card to Thea's apartment, Hermione led them to the back of the resort. She stopped next to two steel doors with a sign that read: Authorized Personnel Only. She inserted a master key card in a reader. The lock on the double doors clicked as they released.

"I thought we were going to my mother's apartment," he said in confusion.

She held the door open for him. "This is the way to the private entrance."

Interesting. They entered a service hallway. So this was the inner workings of the resort. Signs in the hallways clearly marked each entrance to the massive kitchens, to the laundry and to the janitorial services.

"Do you want to go to the apartment alone?" she asked.

Atlas didn't speak, not that he was being rude but rather his vocal cords were frozen. Instead, he shook his head. The last thing he wanted right now was to be alone.

His body filled with dread. The closer they got, the faster his heart pounded. If he was smart, he'd turn around and request that everything in the apartment be disposed of. But he knew it wouldn't be that easy. There would be legal papers and whatnot in the apartment that he, as the heir to his mother's estate, would need to sort out.

At the end of the lengthy hallway was a private elevator. This time he slid the key card that Hermione had given him into the reader. The silver doors silently slid open.

"Are you sure you want to do this?" she asked.

"I have to." His voice was monotone as he refused to let Hermione see just how much this bothered him. He had gotten through worse—like when Thea left him alone with his neglectful father.

On wooden legs, Atlas stepped into the small elevator car. There were no buttons to press as it had only one stop, Thea's apartment. The seconds it took to ride to the third floor were silent as he prepared himself to deal with his mother's things.

The door slid open, and he stared out at the large foyer. It was all done up in white with a large painting of the colorful sunset reflected over the sea to add a splash of color to the room. She certainly did love art.

The glass door leading to the apartment was propped open as though it were always open to visitors. He wondered what his mother would say if she knew he was about to enter her private space.

"Atlas?" When he glanced at Hermione, she asked, "Are you going to step out of the elevator?"

He swallowed hard and then took a step forward. "I never thought I'd be doing this."

All he could surmise about Thea's motives was that since she didn't have any other children, he had become her heir by default. Still, another prick to his scarred heart.

"I'm sorry it's come as such a shock. I have some idea what you're going through."

"Because you lost your mother too?"

She nodded. "When I was seventeen. She had a brain aneurysm. One moment she was fine, the next her head hurt so bad she went to the hospital. I didn't know what was going on at first. Who thinks they'll die from a headache?"

He reached out and took her hand in his. His thumbs gently stroked the back of her hand. He didn't say anything. He didn't know what to say. He felt helpless.

"They…they, um, rushed her to surgery. I never prayed so hard in my life. But…but it had ruptured by the time they got in there. She hung on for a little bit but…"

Her words failed her. She held up a finger as she gathered herself. "When it came time to discuss when to turn off life support, I'd never felt so alone in my life."

Atlas drew her to him. Her cheek came to rest on his chest as his hand slowly and gently rubbed her back. Her arms wrapped around him as though he were an anchor to the present, who kept her from getting swept away in the painful memories of the past. He'd never been someone's anchor before. He liked the feeling of being needed—being able to comfort her in some small way.

She drew in an unsteady breath and then pulled away. "After she died, I lost everything."

For a moment, this wasn't about him. Hermione's loss was so much greater than his. "I'm sorry. That must have been awful."

"It was. My mother was my best friend. I miss her all of the time. I'm sorry you didn't have that closeness with your mother."

He shook his head. "She walked away from me when I was very young."

"I bet she wishes she hadn't done it."

He shrugged. "She came back once years later, but the damage was done by then. I wanted nothing to do with her."

"She never gave up on you."

His gaze swung to her. "Why would you say that?"

"Because she left all of this to you."

He shrugged it off. "That's only because she didn't have any other children."

"Maybe. But I don't think that's the reason. I

think she wanted you to have this place because it brought her such happiness." When he shook his head, refusing to accept what Hermione was saying, she continued. "If she didn't want you to have it, she could have donated it to a worthy cause."

That was true. Maybe Hermione had something there, but in order to accept Hermione's theory, it would mean he'd have to accept the fact that his mother still cared about him. And he wasn't ready to do that. He wasn't ready to forgive and forget.

"Let's see what we have to deal with." He stepped past her and entered the apartment.

The living room was huge. Size-wise it put his penthouse in London to shame. He stepped forward, finding a wall of windows that gave an unobstructed view of the beach. The view was priceless.

"It's beautiful, isn't it?" Hermione stepped up next to him.

"You've seen this view before?"

"I have. Your mother liked to host parties for the staff. She called us her family. After your stepfather died, she felt very alone up here. She spent more and more time working with the staff."

"She didn't have to be alone," he muttered under his breath. He refused to feel sorry for her. She'd made her choices—she'd walked away with barely a glance back.

"I think I see some rays of sunshine poking

through the clouds," Hermione said. "We can go out on the deck."

She led him to the door that opened onto a partially covered deck. They quietly stared out at the sea for a couple of minutes. The sea breeze had warmed up a bit. It was like being on top of the world up here. But he wasn't here to vacation or enjoy the view. He was here to pack up his mother's belongings and dispose of them—just like she'd disposed of him.

"I better get to work." He held the door for Hermione.

Once back inside the living room with its white-and-aquamarine decor, he looked around, taking in all of the artwork from statues to wall hangings. He had no doubt the art in the apartment alone would be worth a fortune. This was going to be more involved than he'd originally thought. Did he auction it all off? Or donate it to the Ludus Gallery?

There were so many decisions to make. What would Thea want? Why hadn't she left detailed instructions? Why did he even care about what she'd want?

His head started to throb. He needed to think about something else—anything else. He turned to Hermione. "How did you come to work here?"

"Your stepfather was the one who hired me after my mother died. I was so happy to no longer be living on the streets that I was willing to do what was asked of me, and that was good enough for him. I started at the front desk and under your mother's guidance I worked my way up to the administrative offices. Then they offered to pay me to go back to school."

"It's impressive. Not everyone could have come through what you did and remained standing. The more I learn about you, the more you amaze me."

He stared into her eyes, seeing the pain those memories brought to her. And then he felt guilty for feeling sorry for himself. From the way he saw it, Hermione had it so much worse than him because she'd not only lost a mother who had loved her, but she'd been homeless. He couldn't imagine how horrific that must have been for her.

"I'm so sorry," he said.

"For what?"

"For acting like I had it rough because my mother rejected me."

Hermione's gaze narrowed in on him. "Don't do that."

"Do what?"

"Feel sorry for me. I'm fine." Her voice took on a hard edge. "I'm taking care of myself. And I haven't done too bad. I don't need you or anyone else feeling sorry for me. Got it?"

He didn't blame her for being defensive. It's probably what got her through those long, cold nights on the street. Sympathy welled up in him.

He held up his hands in surrender. "Got it."

"Now, what is your plan for this place?"

He told her how he wanted everything in the apartment inventoried. And then he would take the list and split it into trash, donations, and at Hermione's insistence there would be a keep category. He didn't want to fight with her so he went along with it, but he already knew there wouldn't be anything he was keeping.

And then they agreed to meet back at the apartment as five o'clock. He realized the sooner he finished his time on the island, the sooner he'd have to say goodbye to Hermione. The thought sat heavy in his chest.

CHAPTER NINE

IT HAD BEEN a rough evening.

At least it had been for Atlas.

In that moment, Hermione did what she'd just yelled at him for—she'd felt sorry for him. But it was different. Really it was.

Going through a parent's belongings no matter how good or bad the relation, it was never easy. It was like an emotional jack-in-the-box. And you just never knew when you opened something what emotions were going to be attached to that particular item.

He'd started working in one of the guest rooms while she set to work in the living room. She'd had the forethought to have Rhea track down some colored stickers to mark items after they were inventoried on their computers. They worked nonstop for a few hours.

When they decided to call it quits for the night, she decided to take him to a late dinner at the Under the Sea restaurant. But when she found it was booked solid, she did something she rarely did—she exerted her executive privilege. Minutes later there was a text message that the best table in the restaurant had just opened up.

"Can't we just order room service?" Atlas asked when she'd prodded him to dress for dinner.

"No. We can't. You came here to see the resort. Consider this part of your tour. Now hurry. We can't be late."

"Why?"

She sighed. "Because I had to pull some strings to get this reservation. With the resort fully booked, reservations are at a premium."

"Which restaurant are we eating at?"

"You'll see." And then she smiled. "Trust me, you'll like it."

Twenty minutes later, she exited her office dressed in a little black dress. After being caught without a change of clothes the night of the storm, she'd decided to keep some outfits in her office. The dress wasn't too fancy. And it wasn't boring either. It was cut to fit her curves as though it were specially made for her.

And then there were the black heels. They were...well, they were stunning. It's the reason she'd splurged on them. And they fit her perfectly. She rarely had an occasion to wear them. But dinner at Under the Sea seemed like the perfect occasion.

Rhea had already gone home for the evening when Atlas had arrived to escort Hermione to dinner. He had relented and changed clothes. He now wore a dark suit with a light purple dress shirt and a vibrant purple tie. It was different and yet it looked quite attractive on him. When her gaze rose and met his, her heart fluttered. It was getting hard to remember that this was a business dinner and not a date.

"You look beautiful." It was though his deep voice caressed her.

Heat swirled in her chest. It rushed up her neck and set her cheeks ablaze. "Thank you. You clean up really well too."

He held his arm out to her. She couldn't remember the last time a man had done that for her. Otis never had. He thought chivalry was a waste of time.

She should resist Atlas's offer and keep a boundary between them because he was far too sexy and he made her pulse race. But she threw caution to the wind as she slipped her hand in the crook of his arm. She noticed the firm muscle beneath her fingertips. Her heart thump-thumped as they set off for the evening.

As they stood in the elevator, he said, "I didn't realize there was a lower level. What's down here?"

"We're going to Under the Sea."

"We're going to look at fish? But I thought we were eating."

She smiled at his frown. "I promise you will eat soon."

The doors swung open into a darkened room. It was more like a wide hallway that had glass walls and ceiling. The glow of the fish tank cast a blue glow over the room. And on each table was an LED candle. There were only a couple dozen tables lining each side of the room.

"This is amazing," Atlas said, gazing all around, taking in the hundreds of fish in all variety of colors. "Did you see that?"

"See what?"

"I think it was a small shark. But I don't see it now."

They were shown to their table, which sat midway down the dining room. It gave them an amazing view of it all. He lifted his head to watch the fish as they swam overhead.

"No wonder you wanted to bring me here," he said in awe, as though he'd totally forgotten what they'd been doing just an hour or so ago in his mother's apartment. "You must eat here often."

"Actually, I've never eaten here."

He glanced across the table at her. "But why not? Don't you like fish?"

"No, it's not that. I think this is amazing." Then she lowered her voice. "Remember I work here."

"Oh. Sorry. Sometimes I forget that employees aren't able to enjoy the amenities. You know, someone really needs to change that rule."

"You mean someone like the owner." She looked expectantly at him.

"Oh, you want me to change the company policy?"

"Well, you do own the resort."

He shook his head. "I don't think you want me changing things."

She arched a brow. "Why not?"

"Because you seem to like everything exactly the way it is. You take comfort in the routine of it all."

She wasn't so sure she liked him trying to figure her out. And even worse, he was right.

"Maybe I do," she said defensively. "But that's because I know what it's like not to know where I was going to sleep at night or where my next meal was coming from." She hadn't intended to admit all of that, but Atlas had a way of burrowing under her skin and she found herself uttering things she preferred to keep to herself.

"I'm sorry." He had the decency to look sheepish. "I never should have said any of that. I was just trying to point out how different we are."

Perhaps she'd overreacted. "And maybe I'm a bit defensive. My ex had criticism down to a fine art by the end of our relationship. I guess I still haven't developed a thick skin."

"Don't. You're perfect just the way you are."

Her cheeks grew warm. "You don't have to say that."

"I meant it." He smiled at her. "I'm so happy I found you—I mean because you've been so helpful."

But the way he looked into her eyes she couldn't help but wonder if he meant something else. Because she was starting to develop feelings for him and she knew that wasn't good. Not good at all.

Once he'd accomplished his business on the island he'd be gone. And she'd be left with nothing but a broken heart. She wouldn't put herself through that again. She just had to keep reminding herself that this candlelit dinner was business. But it sure didn't feel like it.

Dinner was delicious.

The atmosphere was out of this world.

But it was the company that was priceless.

Atlas hadn't thought he would smile again after sorting through Thea's belongings. At the apartment, he'd been reminded of how alone he'd been after his mother had left him.

But now inside this giant aquarium-like room, he was no longer alone. He had Hermione—as a friend, or course. Though they'd only known each other a short time, he didn't know how he'd get through any of this without her.

After their dinner dishes were cleared, he reached across the table and placed his hand over hers. In the candlelight, he stared into her eyes. "Thank you."

"For what? Bringing you here? I'm sure you'd have eventually made it here on your own."

"Not the restaurant—though I am glad you refused to do room service—but rather I meant helping me through this process." As she smiled at him, he gave her hand a squeeze. His gaze dipped to her lips, causing his heart to beat faster. Then realizing what he was doing, he lifted his gaze to meet hers once more. "It means a lot. And I won't forget it. If you ever need anything, all you have to do is phone me."

She withdrew her hand and glanced away.

What had he said wrong? He could speak programming language fluently, but he didn't have a clue how to speak on a personal level to a woman. And he didn't want to mess up this thing they had—this working relationship. Because it wasn't anything more—it couldn't be. He didn't do longterm anything. He liked his freedom—at least that's what he'd been telling himself for years.

"Would you like dessert?" he asked.

She shook her head. "I'm ready to call it a night."

"Not yet." His eyes pleaded with her. "Maybe we could go back to my suite for some coffee. You could tell me more about the resort." When he sensed she was going to reject his invitation, he said, "Please."

She hesitated. "Just a few minutes. I have to get home."

"I understand."

She stood and pushed in her chair. Her gaze never met his. He felt as though he needed to apologize for something, but he just couldn't figure out what it would be.

They quietly made their way back to his suite. Each was lost in their thoughts. Only this time he didn't have a clue what she was thinking.

Inside the suite there was a lamp lit on a side table. It sent a soft glow throughout the living room. They both sat on the couch. Hermione left a great distance between them. For Atlas, it felt as though she were trying to get away from him. And for the life of him, he couldn't figure out what had happened. Whatever he'd said or done, he wanted to take it back. He longed to return things to the way they'd been before the dinner— light and easy.

"I'm sorry if I said or did something wrong at dinner," he said.

"It's okay."

"No, it's not. I don't even know what I did to upset you." He raked his fingers through his hair. "Here's the thing. I'm not very good with speaking to women, you know, on a personal level."

Her gaze met his. "You seem to do just fine with me."

"Really? Because I'm thinking that if I was better at it, you wouldn't be so anxious to get away from me." He leaned back on the couch.

The events of the day weighed heavily on him. "Maybe I shouldn't have drawn you into my nightmare. It wasn't fair of me."

"I don't mind helping you." When he sent her a skeptical look, she said, "I mean it."

"Then what happened between us? Things were going so well, until they weren't." And then he wondered if it was this growing attraction between them that had made things awkward.

"Do you really care what I think?"

"Of course I do."

"Why?"

She wanted him to dissect his feelings and put them into words? His chest tightened. He wasn't good with mushy stuff. But as he gazed into her eyes, he realized that's exactly what she expected. His hands grew clammy.

He cleared his throat. "Because you're my one friend on this island."

She smiled at him. It was the kind of smile that lit up her eyes and made the gold flecks in them twinkle. "Stop overthinking things." Her voice was soft and sultry. "We're good."

He sat upright, rubbing his palms on his pants. He was so anxious to move beyond this awkward moment. "We are?"

She nodded as she continued to smile. "We are."

Maybe there was something to this mushy stuff. When he spoke, his voice came out deeper than he'd intended. "Because when this is all over and I go home, I'm going to miss you."

"You are?"

With his gaze still holding hers, he nodded. "Definitely."

"I'll, ah, miss you too."

His gaze lowered to her lush lips. His heart pounded. As though drawn to her by a force that was beyond his control, he leaned toward her. Surely she had to feel it too. Right? It couldn't just be him.

His eyes closed as his lips pressed to hers. He willed her to kiss him back. Surely he hadn't misread things between them. Had he?

And then her hands reached out, cupping his face. Her touch was feathery soft, as though she was afraid he might disappear in a puff of smoke. Her lips slowly moved over his as she took the lead.

Thoughts of his mother's estate slipped from his mind. Worries over selling the island were swept away. Anxiety about the security of the royal jewels eased. In this moment, his thoughts were only of Hermione and how right this kiss felt.

He wanted this moment to go on and on. Because a kiss was normally just a kiss, a prelude to something more. However, with Hermione, it was all by itself an earthmoving event. His lips gently brushed over hers. He didn't want to scare her off. He wanted to hold her in his arms as long as possible.

As he drew her closer, their kiss intensified. His whole body came alive with the rush of adrenaline. He'd never been so consumed with a kiss.

Hermione was unique in so many wonderful and amazing ways. As her lips moved beneath his, he wondered how he'd been so lucky to meet her.

The reality of their circumstances slipped away. The only thing that mattered right now was him and her. And this kiss that was like a soothing balm on his tattered and torn heart.

He didn't want this moment to end. His hand reached up and gently caressed the smooth skin of her cheek. His fingers slid down to her neck where he felt her rapid pulse. She wanted him as much as she wanted him.

Buzz-buzz.

He didn't want his phone to ruin this moment. He didn't want anything to come between them. It vibrated in his pocket, distracting him from Hermione's tantalizing kiss.

She pulled away. His eyes opened to find her staring at him. He couldn't read her thoughts. Was she happy about the kiss? Or was she angry that he'd overstepped?

She glanced away. "You better answer that. It's probably important. And it's getting late. I'll see you in the morning."

Buzz-buzz.

"But I don't want to answer it. I want us to talk."

She shook her head as she stood. "We've definitely said more than enough for tonight. Good night."

And then she was out the door in a flash. Once more he was left with questions where she was concerned.

Buzz-buzz.

Why wouldn't his phone stop ringing? Surely it must have switched to voice mail by now. He yanked it from his pocket to turn it off, but then he caught sight of the caller ID. It was an important client from London.

Normally, he'd drop everything to answer it. But these weren't normal times. It was his policy to meet problems head-on instead of letting them fester. But this problem wasn't with his client. It was with Hermione.

He'd made a mistake by kissing her. He should have known better, but he'd let himself get caught up in the evening—he'd let himself imagine their dinner had been something more than it was. And now he'd blurred the lines of their relationship.

He needed to focus on business. It didn't confuse him or hurt him. It was a constant that he could always count on. And so when his phone rang again, he answered it.

"Atlas, what's going on?" Krystof practically shouted into the phone.

It was best to find out what he knew before

admitting to anything. "What are you talking about?"

"Don't give me that. You left me this urgent message that we had to talk right away. What's wrong?"

"Everything." He raked his fingers through his hair. "And nothing."

It wasn't the reason he'd left the voice mail. But so much had changed since then, and he needed a friend to speak to. Krystof was a very old friend, someone he could confide in.

"What are you talking about?"

Atlas blew out a deep breath. Suddenly, he wasn't so sure he was ready to discuss Hermione with anyone.

"Nothing. It's just been a long day."

"It's a woman."

"What? No." He suddenly felt self-conscious about this avalanche of emotions for Hermione.

"I'm right. I knew it. What's her name?"

"There's no woman," he snapped. "I mean not really. Anyway, that isn't the reason I called. I think the resort has more to offer you than you think."

"I'm listening."

Atlas went on to tell him all about the casino and the high rollers room. "So how soon can you get here? You'll love it."

"Says the man anxiously trying to unload the island. Sorry. I still can't get there any sooner than next week, and this place better be as good as you say it is."

They wrapped up the phone call with Atlas promising Krystof that he would fall in love with the island.

But as Atlas opened his laptop to go back to work, his thoughts turned to Hermione and their kiss. Had it been a mistake? If it was, it was a delicious one.

CHAPTER TEN

WHY HAD SHE done that?

Why had she kissed him back?

Hermione knew the answer, but she didn't want to admit it to herself or anyone else. The truth was she couldn't quit thinking about that kiss and replaying it over and over in her mind. She was drawn to Atlas in a way that she'd never been drawn to a man in her life—not even her ex. And that scared her.

Even to crack open the door to her heart a little and let Atlas in frightened her. Because every time she opened herself up to care about someone, she lost them. They either disappeared from her life or they ended up not being who she thought they were—except for her Ludus friends. They were always there for her.

And worse yet, Atlas was out to ruin the world she'd immersed herself in here at the Ludus. Sure, he might have promised to protect the employees' jobs for six months, but that protection wouldn't include her.

She understood that the new owner would have a different style and require different management. The thought not only saddened her but scared her. Without Adara, Rhea, Titus and the rest of the Ludus team, she would be all alone again.

And so that night at her apartment instead of sleeping, she worked on her résumé. It needed a lot of updating. And then she went online and set up an account on a professional networking site. She worked late into the night.

Friday morning, she almost slept through her alarm. She rushed through the shower and dressed. She had to get to work early. The employees' future employment hinged on her holding up her end of the bargain. And she refused to give Atlas any reason to void their agreement.

There had to be a way to rewind things. Yes, if they could just pretend the kiss hadn't happened they would be totally fine. They could work together until he left. As anxious as he was to finish cleaning out his mother's apartment, he'd most likely be gone by Valentine's.

Knowing she had to get a move on before a large chunk of the morning slipped by, she jumped in her car and headed for the island. She told herself to focus on her work and not the soul-stirring, heart-fluttering, best ever kiss. Definitely not that.

When she entered the resort, she immediately

turned toward her office. But as she deposited her purse on her desk, she realized she wasn't going to get any work done until she told Atlas what was on her mind.

When she went to his suite, Atlas didn't answer the door. She messaged him and he told her to come on in. He was out on the balcony.

Her stomach knotted up with nervous tension. Maybe this wasn't such a good idea. But it was too late to change her mind. She used her master key card and let herself inside.

Atlas glanced up from his laptop when he heard her step onto the sunny balcony. "Good morning."

"Morning." Hermione didn't smile. "We need to talk."

"Have a seat?" Atlas gestured to the chair next to him.

She opted to sit across the table from him. Coffee was offered and she declined. Hermione's empty stomach churned. She told herself it was nervousness over what she had to say, and it had absolutely nothing to do with her close proximity to the man whose kisses made her go weak in the knees.

"We need to talk about last night," she said.

"Agreed."

His quick, agreeable response surprised her. "It shouldn't have happened. It…it was a mistake."

His gaze searched hers. "Is that what you really think?"

She glanced down at her hands. "I do."

She couldn't let herself fall for him. He was the enemy of sorts—the man who would steal away the life she'd come to cherish, from the monthly luncheons to the friendly greetings in the hallways. Even some of the guests had become friends.

Her ex may have stolen her money as well as her mother's locket, but Atlas was preparing to steal something so much more valuable—the family she'd worked so hard to create. She couldn't bear the thought of having to start over again.

Buzz-buzz.

Hermione glanced at her phone. There was a message from Adara.

Urgent. Need to talk.

What's wrong?

Adara wasn't one to panic. She was really good at taking things in stride. It's what made her so good at her job of concierge.

Where are you?

I'm meeting with Atlas in his suite.

I'll be right there.

"What's wrong?" Atlas asked.

"It's Adara. She says something urgent came up. She's on her way here." She followed him inside the suite.

Knock-knock.

Atlas opened the door. "Come in."

Adara strode into the suite in her navy-and-white skirt suit and high heels. It wasn't so much her actions or the smile she briefly forced on her face but rather the worry reflected in her eyes that had Hermione on alert.

Adara's worried gaze met hers. "It's Nestor. His wife just called. He's in the hospital."

Hermione knew Adara lived near Nestor's family, and she'd become good friends with his wife. "Oh, no. What happened?"

"A heart attack." Adara's voice was filled with emotion. "They're taking him into surgery. His wife said it was touch and go for a while."

"How awful." Her heart went out to Nestor and his family. He was always so reliable and generous. People naturally smiled when they were around him. He put people at ease, and that really helped him do his job of event coordinator.

Adara nodded. "I just can't believe this happened to him."

"His wife wanted us to know he'll be off work for quite a while."

"Tell them not to worry. His job will be waiting for him when he's ready to return."

Adara nodded. "I will. And I don't want to be crude at this moment, but this complicates matters."

Atlas rubbed his fingers over his freshly shaven jaw. "What's complicated?"

Adara's gaze flickered to him and then back to Hermione. "Nestor is supposed to be planning a Valentine's wedding as well as the Valentine's ball. And his assistant just went out on maternity leave."

Hermione inwardly groaned. What was it with this week? Things just kept getting worse.

Her gaze moved to Atlas to see how he was taking the news. If the frown lines marring his handsome face were any indication, he wasn't taking the information very well. He moved to the glass wall and stared off at the sea.

"I can coordinate the party," Hermione said. "But I can't organize the wedding."

Handling the management of the resort in addition to planning an extravagant party wouldn't leave her any spare time, but this wasn't about her. It was about helping a coworker at his most vulnerable time.

Atlas turned to them. "Would you even know where to begin?"

She straightened her shoulders. "I can figure it out."

He shook his head. "This is a big event. Have

you ever planned a party of that size or grandeur?"

Translated to mean that the party was too important to let an amateur handle. He had no faith in her abilities. No wonder he was anxious to sell the place. He was worried she'd destroy the resort.

"No, I haven't but it doesn't mean I can't do it. Nestor was good at keeping notes." She turned to Adara. "Do you know where his company laptop is?"

"As far as I know, he was never without it. It's probably at his house. I can pick it up for you."

"Thank you. It's the key to everything." Upon seeing the doubt reflected in their eyes, Hermione said, "Everyone stop worrying. I can handle it. Most of the plans should already be in place. The trick is the follow-through. You know, making sure everything arrives on time and is put in its place."

"You really think you're up to this?" Adara asked. "It's a lot with everything else you're doing."

"I do." She ignored the flutter of nerves in her stomach. "But what about the wedding?"

"I'll take care of it," Adara said.

"You can't do that. You also have your hands full," Hermione said.

"Listen to who's talking." Adara crossed her arms and arched her brows in challenge. "If you're going to pick up some slack, so am I."

Hermione knew how stubborn her friend could

be. "You're not going to change your mind, are you?"

Adara shook her head. "You know me better than that."

Hermione breathed a little easier. "Okay, now that we have the two big items on his calendar taken care of, I'll have to see what else he has going on."

"And I'll talk to Rhea about setting up a schedule to make sure there's food for Nestor's family," Adara said. "If that's all right with you."

Hermione nodded. "Yes. That's a great idea."

"We could hire a professional party planner," Atlas said. "It'll cost extra at this late date, but it'll be worth it. That's what we'll do. I'll put my assistant on it."

If she had been worried about how she'd stay out of his arms going forward, she didn't have to worry any longer. Anything she'd thought had been started between them had been officially doused with his outright disbelief in her abilities.

Hermione glared at him, but he refused to back down.

"Then I'm no longer needed here." Hermione lifted her chin ever so slightly and strode away.

"Hermione, wait," Atlas called out. "I didn't mean it that way."

He'd meant every word he'd said. Of that she was certain. At every turn, he was questioning her and her choices. The backs of her eyes stung.

She blinked repeatedly, refusing to let on that his words had hurt her. She would not give him that power.

Her steps came quickly. The truth was she wanted to be as far from Atlas as she could get. The man utterly frustrated her. One minute he's kissing her like he never wanted to stop—like she was the most beautiful woman in the world.

The next moment he's insulting her abilities. No wonder she hadn't been in a relationship in a long time. Men were utterly exasperating—most especially Atlas.

She walked out the door. She gave it a firm yank but with its gentle close feature, she wasn't given the satisfaction of it slamming closed.

What had he done?

He'd totally messed up everything.

Atlas had watched the storm clouds gather in Hermione's eyes and he hadn't done anything to calm the waters. The reasons—the good reasons—had all been there in his head. But had he used the right words? No.

It seemed that whenever he was in close proximity to Hermione that his mind and mouth had a glitchy disconnect. There were so many things he wanted to say to her, but for one reason or another he'd kept them to himself.

But he couldn't let things stay like this. He couldn't stand the thought of Hermione being upset with him and jumping to the wrong conclusions. He had to fix things or at least try.

After apologizing to Adara, he rushed to the hallway, finding no sign of her. Would she go back to her office? Or would she walk out the front door and keep on going?

Stop. He was getting ahead of himself. After all, she was an employee of the resort. Her address was on record. He could easily track her down if he was so inclined.

Who was he kidding? He was most definitely inclined. He just wasn't sure it was a good idea. After the kiss last night, he knew the volatile attraction ran both ways. He also knew Hermione was in denial of their chemistry. Whether they wanted to admit it or not, it existed.

If he was to go after her now and things got heated—if their attraction spiraled out of control, she'd never forgive him. He wouldn't forgive himself. Things needed to cool off, and then they could talk like rational adults.

After calming down, hopefully she'd see the merits of his plan. She was overextending herself. At the same time, it impressed him the way she was worried about those around her and asked for nothing for herself. There weren't many people that were so selfless.

He returned to his suite where Adara was checking messages on her phone. She glanced up when he entered the room. She slipped her phone in her pocket.

"I didn't handle that very well," he said.

"Did you have a chance to speak to her?"

He shook his head. "I didn't catch up with her."

He sunk down into the chair. "When I came to Ludus I knew it wasn't going to be fun, but I didn't expect things to keep getting worse at every turn."

Adara paused as though not sure she should say what was on her mind. When her phone buzzed, she checked it and then returned it to her pocket.

"It's okay," he said. "Just say it."

"I think you should let Hermione decide how much she can handle. She'll ask for help before she does anything to damage the resort. She loves this place. It's her home—her family. And we won't let her fail. We'll help her every step of the way."

It sounded nice, but he wasn't sure it was based in reality. "Even though it would be above and beyond everyone's duties?"

"Even then. This group pulls together to help each other."

His business didn't run on such employee devotion. This resort was so different from anything he knew. It was a good thing he was selling it because he knew his management style would clash with the established routine.

"The guests will be unhappy if the party goes

awry." When Adara sent him a surprised look, he said, "I've heard them talking in the hallways. This place is abuzz with excitement."

"And you should know that Nestor does have a couple of other staff members. I'm sure they'll pitch in so the party isn't overwhelming for Hermione. And like I said, if more help is required the resort is full of people who would lend a hand."

This whole thing made him uneasy. There was a resort full of famous and influential people who were waiting for a splashy and impressive party. If the party was a failure, it would really hurt the resort's reputation and hamper any potential sale.

He rubbed his jaw. "Even if I could find Hermione, I don't think she'd be willing to hear me out."

Adara sent him a smile. "I think you underestimate yourself. But you have given me an idea."

He braced himself. "Do I even want to know what it is?"

"Don't worry about it. Just go talk to Hermione."

"I don't know where she went."

Adara held up her phone. "But I do. She texted me and mentioned she was stopping by Thea's apartment."

"Really?" Even though Hermione was upset with him, she was still holding up her end of their agreement. He didn't know it was possible, but she impressed him even more.

"Now I have to go." Adara started for the door but then paused to say, "Good luck."

He was going to need it. Hermione had never been this upset with him. And he had no idea how to make it up to her. But that wouldn't stop him from trying.

CHAPTER ELEVEN

SOME PEOPLE WOULD say she was foolish.

Other people would say she was smart.

Hermione really didn't care what people thought of her—well, that wasn't quite true. She cared what Atlas thought. The truth was she cared too much.

She should be in her office right now, but she was too worked up to sit still. She needed some physical activity. She needed to work off some of her frustration.

Hermione carried a stack of books from the bookcase in Thea's living room to the coffee table. There she opened each one, turned it over and shook it to make sure there were no loose papers tucked inside. And then she placed them in a cardboard box to donate as Atlas had instructed.

Though it nearly killed Hermione to admit it, Atlas was right. She couldn't do everything—even if she wanted to. Delegating was the only way she could get through the next week leading up to Valentine's.

She'd had Rhea on speakerphone going over a couple of urgent matters, including the double-booking of the Cypress Room. Once that was sorted, she asked Rhea to temporarily take on some more responsibilities. Her assistant understood that this was a difficult time for the resort and enthusiastically offered to pitch in.

Rhea's kindness and generosity brought tears to Hermione's eyes. Thank goodness they were on the phone. Hermione wasn't usually overly emotional. She blamed the tears on Atlas.

When she disconnected the call, she continued to mull over the scene with Atlas. If she didn't care for Atlas, would his lack of faith in her abilities hurt so much? Unwilling to answer that question, she told herself it was a pride thing. However, deep down she knew it was more than that. She wanted him to be different from her ex, who was always handy with a backhanded compliment. She wanted Atlas to see her as an equal—someone he could share more than a passing moment with—

The breath caught in her lungs. What was she thinking? She was not falling for Atlas. Absolutely not.

"Hermione?" Atlas's voice carried from the elevator into the living room.

She hesitated to answer. If she remained quiet, would he go away? No. Atlas was way too determined when he wanted something. And she would not let him think she was afraid to face him.

"In here." She would just treat him like any other coworker.

The sound of his approaching footsteps echoed in the foyer. And then he was there, filling up the doorway with his broad shoulders. "Can we talk?"

"Now isn't a good time. I'm a little busy." She continued opening books, shaking them and placing them in the box.

It was the same way she'd act with any other coworker. But any other person wouldn't make her heart race just by their presence.

Just ignore it. He'll be gone soon.

"This is important."

She stopped working. Hesitantly her gaze met his. "So is this. I have my end of a bargain to keep. And the sooner I finish, the sooner we'll no longer have to deal with each other."

He sighed. "Hermione, you took what I said out of context—"

"I don't think so." She resumed her task.

Buzz-buzz.

Her gaze moved to her phone, resting on the cherrywood end table. It wasn't her phone. That meant it had to be Atlas's, and she'd never been so grateful for an interruption. His phone went off again. She willed him to answer it.

"I need to get this, but we're not done talking."

She didn't say anything, but she was thinking plenty. None of her testy thoughts would make this situation any easier.

He stepped into the foyer to take the call. He didn't say much. Most of the conversation appeared to be one-sided. Then he stepped back in the study. "I have to go take care of something, but I'll be back."

"Don't rush on my account."

He hesitated as though he were going to say something, but then he'd thought better of it. He walked away, and at last she could take a full breath.

She had to quit letting him get to her. After all, it wasn't like they were a couple or anything. She needed to work faster because once Nestor's laptop was delivered to the resort, she would need to focus most of her energies on the Valentine's ball.

She continued her task with renewed determination. After quickly moving through a dozen or so books, her phone rang. She had no intention of answering it, especially if it was Atlas. But curiosity had her checking the caller ID.

When she saw Adara's name on the screen, she couldn't help but wonder what she would need. Perhaps the laptop had already arrived. She was anxious to see exactly what party details needed to be completed. It would be a lot as no detail was overlooked or extravagance forsaken when it came to a Ludus event. They were the definition of lavish.

She pressed the phone to her ear. "Hello."

"Hermione, I'm so sorry to bother you, but there's a problem at the dock. It's something about a special shipment for the party, and they're insisting on your signature."

Hermione inwardly groaned. This was the last interruption she needed at the moment. Her gaze moved around the study. It wasn't like the work wouldn't be here when she got back.

"Okay. I'm on my way."

Adara gave her the instructions and then hung up. It all seemed easy enough. And with it being an unusually warm, sunny day, it'd be a good day for a walk. It would be a chance for her to clear her mind and figure out how to deal with Atlas in a calm, reasonable manner.

A strange place for a meeting.

Atlas sat aboard the resort's luxury yacht—*The Sea Jewel*. Adara had phoned him and asked him to meet her there. She'd sounded anxious or worried; he wasn't quite sure which but something was definitely not right with her.

He was starting to worry about the resort. Without his mother at the helm, would the service decline? Hermione seemed good at her job, but she was getting spread too thin.

The problem was that she was too fiercely independent for her own good, and that could spell trouble for the resort. And he wouldn't be of much help. He didn't know a thing about running a resort, but he did know how to manage people. Still, his style of management and hers were two very different things.

Should he step in and assume control of the resort? It was the very last thing he wanted to do. He'd only come here to settle his mother's personal affairs and now he felt as though he was being drawn in more deeply with every passing hour.

The captain escorted Atlas to the interior of the boat. It was spacious and appeared to have every amenity a person could want, from long comfy white couches to captain chairs along with a large bar and a giant screen television.

Atlas sat down on the couch but unable to sit still for long, he started pacing. He was forever staring out the long bank of windows, hoping someone would arrive soon.

Tired of waiting, he reached for his phone. There must have been some sort of mix-up. He would call Adara and find out what was going on. His finger hovered over the screen when he detected movement on the dock. *At last.*

He slipped the phone back in his pocket. He headed for the deck to greet Adara and get down to business. But when he stepped outside, he was greeted by Hermione.

When her gaze met his, her eyes widened. "What are you doing here?"

"That's just what I was going to ask you."

"I was told I needed to sign for a shipment, but when I got to the dock, I was guided onboard the yacht." Her brows drew together. "I don't understand. Why are you here?"

"I was told to meet Adara here, but I haven't seen her."

Hermione crossed her arms. "What's going on? I don't have time to play games."

He had a suspicion who might be behind this setup. "Who called you?"

"Adara." Hermione's brows rose as her eyes lit up. "Let me guess. She called you too?"

"Yes. It looks like she set us up."

As though in confirmation, the engine started. The boat started to move away from the dock.

"Hey!" Hermione called out. "Wait."

Atlas shook his head. "They can't hear you."

"What are we going to do?"

"Apparently we're going for a ride." It was certainly one way to obtain Hermione's undivided attention. He just didn't know if this cruise would be long enough for him to convince her to forgive him.

"But…but that's kidnapping." Hermione frowned. "I have work to do. I don't have time to go sailing." She turned to him. "Are you just going to stand there?"

"I was actually thinking of sitting down and enjoying the view." And he did just that.

"You can't be happy about this."

"I will definitely have a word with Adara when we get back." He would thank her for this terrific idea, but next time he wanted to be clued in on her plans ahead of time. Then he was going to give her a well-deserved raise.

Hermione huffed. "You could tell the captain to turn around right now."

Perhaps a change of subject would help. "I didn't know the resort owned a yacht."

"They own many boats but not all are this fancy. This one is brand-new. Your mother ordered it just before she...well, uh, it was just delivered." She looked flustered as she avoided his gaze.

"What you're saying is that we're the first ones to ride in it?"

She shrugged. "I don't know for sure, but I think so. It'll come in handy come June."

"What's in June?"

"The Royal Regatta."

He was intrigued. And the more Hermione talked about the resort the less stiff her posture became. "What does it entail?"

She sat down. "It's a boat race around the island."

He joined her. "And who participates in this race?"

"A lot of people—even the prince of Rydiania. It's his country that cosponsors the race."

"The same country that loaned the resort the Ruby Heart and the other jewels?" When she nodded, he asked, "Why would a foreign country lend the resort what must be priceless gems? I thought Thea's husband had been thrown out of the family and exiled to this island."

"That's not quite how it went down. Even though Georgios had been exiled from his homeland of Rydiania, he was free to travel the world—to make his home wherever he pleased. However, his family preferred that it was a long way from Rydiania."

The more Hermione talked, the more her voice took on its normal bubbly lilt. Her arms now rested at her sides. And the frown lines had smoothed from her face.

"And he picked this island of all places to live?" Atlas didn't want her to stop talking about the island and its history because when she was unveiling the past for him, she wasn't thinking about how angry she was with him.

"Georgios said it was love at first sight. He knew once he stepped on the island that he was home. But he quickly grew lonely, and that's when he got the idea to invest his savings into building the Ludus Resort. He said he never regretted that decision."

"If I had a private island," Atlas said, "I don't know if I'd want to share it."

"But you do have an island. Remember? This is all yours."

"It doesn't feel like it."

"What does it feel like?"

"Some sort of messed-up dream and soon I'll wake up."

"But this is no dream. It's your future—if you want it to be."

He didn't want to think about that now. He'd rather enjoy this truce he'd somehow struck with Hermione. "I'm still confused. If this king was cast out of the family—"

"He wasn't cast out. He abdicated the throne. He said he wasn't meant to be a king. He believed his brother could do a better job."

"Still, he was exiled from the country, so why would they lend their jewels?"

Hermione smiled. "Well, that's another story. The current king and queen of Rydiania have three children. The oldest being Prince Istvan. He had known Georgios when he was very young. You might say those two hit it off. When Georgios was exiled, the prince was deeply upset. The king and queen forbade him from contacting his uncle. But you know how kids can be when they're forbidden to do something."

He thought back over his own troubled youth. "It makes the temptation even greater."

"Exactly. When the prince was old enough to travel without his parents or chaperones, he sought out his uncle. To hear it told, and to have witnessed them together, it's like the two had never been parted all of those years."

"And so all was forgiven with Georgios?" He was hoping there would be a happy ending. He needed to know all families weren't messy and broken like his.

"No. I'm afraid not. Georgios said it was enough to have the prince back in his life, but every now and then when he didn't think anyone was looking, he would get this faraway look in his eyes and then a sadness would come over him."

"So much for a happy ending."

"Oh, I think for the most part Georgios was happy. It was just when he thought of his brother that he realized what he'd lost. And as for the royal jewels, they belong to Prince Istvan. He inherited them from his grandmother. He loved your mother and visited often after his uncle passed on. He knew how much your mother loved Valentine's and thought the jewels might cheer her up."

And yet another person Thea had won over. It would appear he and his father were the only two she didn't care for. The thought weighed heavy on him. Was he too much like his father?

"Now that you know the backstory on the jewels, it's time to turn this boat around. I can't believe Adara would do this." She reached for her phone.

"Don't do that. It's a beautiful day." He stood and moved out to the deck. "Why not enjoy some of it?"

"Atlas, we can't just run off for the day. We have things to do." She followed him.

The sea breeze combed through his hair and rushed past his face, offsetting the warmth of the sun. But Atlas didn't pay much attention. He was drawn to the emerging landscape.

"This is beautiful." He stared back at the rocky shoreline with its lush green foliage. "Is that a waterfall off in the distance?"

"Yes. It's one of them. If you want you could explore the island."

He shook his head. "I have too much work to do."

"You should see it during the summer when the orchids and wildflowers are in bloom. It's a cascade of color."

He opened his mouth to say that he couldn't wait to see it but then wordlessly pressed his lips back together. He wouldn't be here come summertime. By then Ludus Island would be in this rearview mirror...where it belonged.

He swallowed. "So the only thing on the entire island is the resort?"

She nodded. "This all belonged to Georgios. He liked having the ability to keep the paparazzi at a distance so he and his guests could enjoy the island's beauty."

"Do you offer sightseeing boat rides for the guests?"

"No, we don't. But now that you mention it, perhaps we could work on putting together something. Maybe a lunch and dinner cruise."

"I'm glad we have this moment together."

She arched a brow. "Don't go thinking any of this erases what happened earlier."

"Will you at least let me explain?"

She didn't say anything at first, then she sighed. "Fine. It's not like I have anyplace I can go. And I don't plan to swim back to shore."

"Back at the suite, the things I said didn't come out right."

"It sounded pretty clear to me. You don't trust me to organize the Valentine's ball. All I'm good for is to clean your mother's apartment."

"Whoa. Where did that come from?"

"Isn't that what you're thinking? That I'm not cut out to run this resort?"

He shook his head. "I never thought such a thing. Who put these thoughts in your head?" When she didn't respond, he said softly, "Hermione, talk to me. What's going on?"

"My ex, Otis, was always planting doubts in my mind. Just little things here and there when I went back to school. At first I didn't pay much attention. It wasn't until Adara pointed out how his little comments over time had eaten away at my self-confidence until I doubted myself about almost everything that I realized he was jealous of my career."

Anger balled up in his gut over what that jerk had done to her. Who did such a thing to such a smart, accomplished and caring person like Hermione?

And then he recalled all of his questions and suggestions for the resort. He'd also insisted on upgrading the resort's security over her objection. And finally he'd questioned her ability to take over the Valentine's party on top of all her other responsibilities. Not because he didn't think she could do it but rather because he cared if she took on too much work.

He cared.

The revelation echoed in his mind. It'd been so long since he'd allowed himself to get close enough to a person to truly care about them. In the process, he'd totally messed up everything.

His gaze met hers. "Hermione, I'm not like your ex."

Disbelief reflected in her eyes. "It doesn't matter—"

"It does matter." His voice was soft but firm. "I know I haven't handled any of this correctly." He needed her to truly hear him. That would only happen if he put himself out there and revealed things he'd never shared with anyone. "Coming to this island—Thea's home—is the hardest thing I've ever done." His voice grew gravelly with emotion. He cleared his throat. "And then to find out how much she cared for all of you… it was hard."

Pity reflected in Hermione's eyes. "I'm so sorry. I should have been more sensitive."

"Don't pity me. I'm fine." He didn't feel fine. He felt beaten and scarred. "I've been caring for myself since I was a kid. I'll get through this."

"You don't have to get through this alone. You could let people in."

He shook his head. The thought of setting himself up to be abandoned like his mother had done or rejected like his father had ultimately done made his protective wall come back up.

"I… I can't talk about this." He strode back inside the yacht.

Hermione followed him. "Running from your past isn't working. Once you face it, it won't have any control over you."

"That's not what I'm doing. I only mentioned it because I'm trying to explain the reason I said and did certain things when I arrived. Instead of telling you what I intended to do, I should have asked for your input. Like the security system we're supposed to work on tomorrow. Do you feel it's too much for the resort?"

Her eyes momentarily widened. "We haven't had problems in the past but what you said got me to thinking. If the resort is to grow, it's feasible to update the security. Just don't go too overboard. We're still just a small island resort."

"Thank you for your input. I'll do my best to run my ideas for the resort past you. My input wasn't meant to demean your capabilities. They were about me and my need to prove myself... that Thea was wrong to leave me—to forget me."

"But she didn't. She loved you—"

"No." His voice came out harshly. He made an effort to soften his tone when he spoke again. "Don't say that. People who love you don't abandon you."

He was losing track of this conversation. Why did he keep revealing more and more of himself? This conversation was supposed to be about Hermione, not him.

He sighed. "I'm saying this all wrong."

Her gaze narrowed in on him. "What exactly are you saying?"

"I'm saying I think you're capable of anything you set your mind to, but I didn't want you to take on too much. As it is, I think you should stop working on Thea's apartment so you can focus on the party. Just promise me one thing."

"What's that?"

"If it's too much or you need help that you'll tell me."

"I'll tell you. But don't worry, I've got this. This is going to be the best party ever." And that's when she leaned into him, wrapping her arms around him as she hugged him.

His heart immediately started to hammer against his ribs. His body froze. He was afraid to move or breathe for fear that she'd pull away. Because having her so close was the most amazing feeling that caused a warm spot in his chest.

When at last she pulled away, he said, "Hermione, I—"

She pressed her fingertips to his lips. "Maybe we've done enough talking."

What? There were still things he wanted to say. But when she moved her fingers from his lips, those words escaped him. What exactly did she have in mind? As though in answer, she pressed her mouth to his. He liked the way she thought.

It wasn't a slow and gentle kiss. No, this was a kiss full of need and longing. Her hand slid up over his shoulder and around his neck until her fingertips raked through his hair. It was the most exhilarating feeling. Desire pumped through his veins.

The right and wrong of their intimacy was long forgotten. A driving need to feel her next to him pulsed through his veins. He wanted to explore all of her. He wanted to make her moan with pleasure.

He scooped her up in his arms. He carried her to the spacious chaise longue and gently laid her down. He joined her. His fingertips swept the loose strands of hair behind her ear.

"Does this mean I'm forgiven?" he murmured.

"Obviously I haven't been doing something right if you have to ask that question. Maybe I should try again." Her eyes twinkled with merriment.

A slow smile pulled at his lips. "Yes, I think we need some definite clarification."

She reached out to him. The backs of her fingers caressed his jawline as desire burned in her eyes. A bolt of need shot through his body.

He'd never had an afternoon tryst. Afternoons had always been for doing business. But with Hermione in his arms business was the last thing on his mind.

CHAPTER TWELVE

HER FEET DIDN'T touch the ground.

At least that's the way it felt.

Hermione's steps were light and quick as she made her way back to the office. She'd never felt this happy—this alive—this, ugh, she ran out of adjectives. Her brain was abuzz with images of being held in Atlas's arms as they'd made love. She had no idea he could be so gentle and loving.

There was so much more to him than she'd ever imagined. She could talk to him—really talk to him. And she felt safe when she confided in him that he wouldn't tell anyone else or use it against her—like Otis had done.

The thought of her ex weighed down her steps. Coming back down to earth, she recalled how excited and certain she'd been of Otis in the beginning. And look how wrong she'd been.

Was she wrong about Atlas too? After all, he still hadn't said he was going to change his mind about selling the resort. But with every passing day, she could see that he was getting more comfortable on Ludus Island. Soon he would realize that it was his destination.

The last thought buoyed her heart once more. It was like his presence on the island was his destiny. He just needed a little more time to figure things out.

Adara headed down the hallway toward her. "I was looking for you."

"Like you didn't know where I was since you're the one who had us whisked away on the yacht." Hermione knew she should be upset with her, but it was so hard when all she wanted to do was smile.

Adara acted as though she hadn't heard her. "I just talked to Nestor's wife and the surgery was a success. Now all he has to do is recover."

"That's the best news I've heard all day. If they need anything, let me know." Hermione was so happy for Nestor and his family. But she wasn't quite done with Adara. "You know I should be really mad at you for pulling that stunt with the boat."

Adara smiled. "But you're not because it worked. You two made up…didn't you?"

"I'm not going to tell you." Hermione resumed walking toward her office. "I can't believe you set us up—set me up. I thought we were friends."

Adara's smile faltered. "We are friends. I… I thought I was helping, but now you've got me worried that it went all wrong."

Hermione chanced a glance at her friend. "You should be worried. That was a very awkward situation."

"Oh." Her shoulders dropped. "So it didn't go well. I'm sorry. I won't do it again. I was just trying to help."

"Actually, it went very well." Hermione smiled.

Adara's eyes widened. "It did?"

"Yes, but you still shouldn't have done it."

"It just felt like you both needed a push, no, make that a shove in the right direction. I've seen the way you two look at each other when you think the other isn't looking. And you've both got it bad."

Her heart did a leap of joy. Atlas was checking her out. "We talked. And we worked some things out."

"Is that what we're calling it these days?" Adara grinned.

Heat flared in Hermione's cheeks. "We aren't discussing that. And I really do have to get back to work. I wasn't expecting to take a boat ride in the middle of the workday."

"So does mean you two are officially a couple now?"

"I… I don't know." They hadn't gotten that far, but she'd like to think they were. There's no way he'd confided in her and then made love to her without feeling anything. But as for labels for their relationship, it was all too new.

"Just be careful around the Ruby Heart. I just saw it—alone, thank goodness—because there's some legend if lovers view it together that their lives will forever be entwined."

Hermione was starting to wonder if there was something to that legend. She wasn't ready to reveal that she'd viewed it with Atlas. "Do you believe it?"

Adara shrugged. "I've heard of stranger things. Why? Are you planning to visit the ruby with Atlas?"

"Stop trying to matchmake."

"But you're totally into him, aren't you?" Adara sent her a hopeful look.

Hermione hesitated. It was as though once she spoke the words it would make not only them but this whole thing with Atlas real. But she knew how silly that was because nothing could have been more real than the love they'd made on the yacht.

With her heart hammering with excitement mixed with a little fear, she said, "Yes." It was barely more than a whisper. She swallowed hard. If she was going to do this, she had to believe in it—in them. "Yes," she said with more force. "How could I not be? Have you looked at him?"

Adara nodded. "He's hot. Does he have a brother?"

"I'm afraid not. He's one of a kind."

Adara sighed. "I guess it's good that I'm happy with my life just the way it is."

Hermione wondered if her friend was as happy with her single status as she'd like others to believe. But considering that Hermione was about to put her tattered heart back out on the line for a man that didn't even live here, much less in the same country, well, she might not be the best person to give relationship advice.

When Monday rolled around, she still couldn't stop smiling.

Hermione felt like she was walking on air ever since Friday when they'd returned from that very special boat ride. She and Atlas had come to a new understanding. They hadn't made love again—not that she hadn't thought of it—but they'd shared meals and updates on their day.

It was as though a wall had come down and they were able to really communicate. She did notice that he didn't mention their relationship or what happened on the boat, but she also knew he was under a lot of stress with having to clean out Thea's apartment.

And though he hadn't spoken of their future or the resort's future, she told herself they still had time. She couldn't rush things—even though that's exactly what she wanted to do.

With each passing day, he was getting more involved in the resort. She shouldn't have doubted that the island would work its charms on him. At this moment, he was off meeting with his security team as they began installing a new state-of-the-art security system. He wasn't one to pass off tasks to others; he was overseeing this installation personally.

But now with the party at the end of the week, she had to focus fully on the preparations. Thankfully Nestor had everything well organized. Her main tasks were to make sure the ballroom had been cleaned from top to bottom and then verify everything had been delivered.

"How's it going?" Atlas stood in the doorway of the event coordinator's office.

She looked up from where she sat behind Nestor's desk. "I just finished a phone call to make sure the ice sculpture would be here on time."

"And what did you learn?"

"It will be here early and stored in our walk-in freezer. Nestor made this job very easy for me."

Atlas lounged against the doorjamb. "Don't go jinxing yourself. You still have a lot to do before everything is set to go."

"I know." She stood up and moved toward him. "But I think a positive attitude is half the battle."

He nodded in agreement. "It's nice to see you

in such a good mood." His voice took on a serious tone. "But I have something to ask you."

"Uh-oh." Her mind raced. "If this is about Thea's apartment, don't worry. I'll get back to it after the party. I never meant to pull out of our agreement."

He shook his head. "That isn't it. I have a special guest flying in for the party, and I need to know if there is anywhere for him to stay?"

"No. I'm sorry. The resort is fully booked. The Valentine's ball is always a big draw." She gave the idea some thought. "There's the spare room in your suite."

"I thought of that, but I'm not sure that's the right impression I want to give him of the resort. And I don't know if he'll be traveling alone."

"What about putting them in Thea's apartment?"

Once again Atlas shook his head. Then he sighed. "But I could move there and give him the suite."

She knew he'd had a very complicated relationship with his mother. She also knew he was happier when he spent the least amount of time in Thea's apartment. This couldn't be easy for him. This guest must be very important to him.

And then she thought of an idea. "Or you could stay on the mainland at my flat."

He sent her a barely there smile. "Thank you

for the offer. But I need to spend more time sorting Thea's things. If I'm staying there, I won't be able to procrastinate nearly as much."

She nodded. "I understand. I'll have your things moved—"

"Don't worry. I have it under control."

When he didn't move on, she asked, "Did you need something else?"

"I just noticed that with the nicer weather more people are gravitating outdoors." He opened his mouth as though he wanted to say more but then wordlessly closed it.

"When the weather warms up, it's even busier. And the regatta draws a huge crowd."

"Interesting. It'd probably be an even larger crowd if the resort wasn't for select clientele."

"You mean rich people."

"Yes. I'm just not sure why my mother hadn't changed it. I don't recall her being all about status. But then again, I was just a little kid when I knew her. What did I know back then?"

"I'm only guessing, but something tells me your mother kept the resort the same because it's the way her late husband liked it. And it really is nice the way it is. Give it a chance. It'll grow on you."

"I don't know." *Buzz-buzz.* He glanced at his phone. "I've got to get this. We'll talk more later."

And then he was gone. She didn't know what to

think about what he'd suggested. Why would she change things when she loved them as is? Was it possible the island hadn't worked its charms on Atlas like she'd hoped? And if so, where did that leave her?

CHAPTER THIRTEEN

HE DIDN'T KNOW how to act around her.

Atlas could see that their lovemaking had changed things for Hermione. She no longer looked at him like he was the enemy—out to destroy the traditions of the Ludus.

But had things changed for him? He didn't think so. He was still moving ahead with the sale of the resort. But when it came to Hermione, all he wanted to do was to pull her into his arms and hold her close. Still, he resisted the idea because when he left the island, he didn't want to hurt her.

And since she hadn't mentioned their lovemaking, neither had he. He wouldn't know what to say—hey, it was amazing but a mistake. He couldn't say that to her, especially after knowing how her ex had treated her.

Instead, he'd kept a respectable distance from her. It wasn't helping because he noticed that she looked at him differently now, like she was caressing him with her gaze. And the way she spoke was of a softer tone, not to mention her agreeable attitude.

He wasn't much better. When he'd sought her out earlier, he'd almost asked her to go strolling on the beach with him. He couldn't imagine anything better than her hand in his with a gentle sea breeze as the sun warmed their faces.

But then he wondered what sort of idea that would give her. It was the sort of thing couples did. Was that what he wanted?

No. He was terrible with any sort of relationship; just ask any of the women who'd passed through his life.

The only thing he knew to do was to throw himself into upgrading the resort's security. Once that was completed, he would spend all of his time working on Thea's apartment because he couldn't stay here forever.

It was late by the time he and his team finished working for the day. He fully expected Hermione to have gone home by then, but when he strolled by her office, she was so immersed in her work that she didn't notice him at her doorway until he knocked.

"Hey, it's time to call it a night." He stepped into the office, automatically pulling the door shut behind him.

"I still have so much to do." Her gaze moved over the various stacks of papers and files on her desk.

He glanced around her desk, noticing that it wasn't as neat and tidy as it'd been when he'd first arrived.

"And it will wait until tomorrow." He couldn't believe he had just uttered those words.

He was a certified workaholic. But the more time he spent on this island, the more he was finding an interest in things other than work such as spending as many meals with Hermione as their busy schedules allowed.

She sighed. "Maybe you're right." She began shutting down her computer. "It has been a long day."

"Do you have a moment before you go home?" He'd missed spending time with her and hoped she wouldn't rush off.

"Sure. What do you need?"

"I have something I want to show you." He'd found a photo album full of Ludus employees, and he'd thought Hermione would know what to do with it.

After she gathered her things, she said, "Let's go."

"Right this way." He opened the door for her.

As they walked, she asked, "Did you eat?"

He cleared his throat. "I had something with the guys." And then he worried she'd waited for him. "Did you eat?"

She nodded. "I wasn't sure how late you'd be."

"There was a lot to do, and there were a couple of problems with the installation. In order to have it all up and running by the unveiling of the Ruby Heart on Valentine's, we had to work late." He rubbed the back of his neck.

For a while, they walked in a peaceful quietness. He couldn't help but wonder if this was what it was like for couples after a long day. Did they quietly enjoy each other's presence without having to speak?

He chanced a glance at Hermione as they took the private elevator to Thea's apartment. Her face was drawn with exhaustion and he had an urge to step in and take over the party planning, but he knew that was the last thing Hermione would want. She had promised to say something if it was too much. He had to trust her.

Once in the apartment, he gestured to the couch. "Why don't you come sit down?"

He took a seat next to her. "How's the party prep coming?"

"Good. The ballroom was cleaned until it gleamed. Tables have been set up. Tomorrow we'll start decorating."

"Is there anything I can do?"

She shook her head. "I've got this."

"I do have a question for you. My friend Krystof Mikos arrives tomorrow, and he's very interested in getting a seat at the high-stakes poker game. Is that possible?"

"Sure it is. I'll have Adara make the arrangements." She wrote a note and then paused. "The buy-in won't be a problem for your friend, will it?"

"Not at all." Krystof had more money than a small country, but he didn't act like it.

"Are you sure you wouldn't like to try your hand at cards?"

He shook his head again. "I only take chances on sure things."

"You mean your business?"

"Yes."

"And what about us?" Her gaze searched his. "Are we a sure thing?"

At last she'd broached the ominous subject weighing over them. The word *yes* teetered on the tip of his tongue, surprising him with his willingness to involve himself in a relationship. He bit back the answer. It was a moment of delusion—a moment when he wanted to believe that happily-ever-after truly existed.

It was Hermione's fault. She made him want to believe in fairy tales and happy endings. The last thing he should do was get anywhere near her.

The memories of their lovemaking were always there, lurking at the edge of his thoughts. And getting close to her would be too tempting. He'd want to pull her close and continue where they'd left off.

But that would be wrong. He couldn't offer her anything but a good time. And Hermione didn't strike him as the type to have a casual relationship. When she cared about people, she put her whole heart on the line.

"Listen, I've been meaning to talk to you but there just wasn't a chance earlier." He struggled to find the right words.

"I wanted to talk to you too. I don't want to rush things."

"Rush things?"

"With us. I've done that before. I led with my heart instead of my head, and it didn't go well."

He didn't like being grouped with her jerk of an ex. "I'm not your ex."

"I know that. It wasn't what I meant." The pained look in her eyes said her ex had hurt her worse than she was letting on. "Otis was handsome and said all of the right words. And he happened into my life just when I needed someone."

"Sounds like you cared a lot about him." An uneasy feeling snaked its way through him.

"I did. At least in the beginning. I thought—well, I hoped he'd fill the hole that my mother's death had left in my heart. The emptiness. The loneliness. It was just so much. When Otis came along, he flirted with me and flattered me. I thought it was meant to be."

The uneasy feeling swelled within him. "You were happy?"

She nodded. "For a time."

"And then what happened?"

"He lost his job. When he had problems finding another one, he grew jealous of my education and my career. Somewhere along the way he stopped looking for work. He sponged off me and then took my money to the bar where he bought rounds of drinks for his friends."

"That must have been rough."

She shrugged. "It wasn't the best, but I thought it was a bad spell and we'd work through it so I put up with it for a time. But even I have my limits. I kicked him out. He stole all of my money and the few pieces of my mother's jewelry before he skipped town."

"That's horrible." Anger replaced the jealousy that had coiled up in his gut. "Who does such a thing?"

She shook her head. "It doesn't matter. It's over. I just wish I could get my mother's heart-shaped locket back. I tried every pawnshop I could find but none had it."

He hoped he never met this Otis guy. It wouldn't be good for either one of them. Though it would make Atlas feel a bit better to knock some sense into the guy.

"What did the locket look like?" he asked.

"I have a picture of it." She pulled out her phone. Her finger rapidly moved over the screen. And then she held up a photo of her wearing the locket.

He took the phone from her and enlarged the

photo. It was a heart locket with an intricate engraved design. And in the center was a ruby.

Who would steal the necklace of a dead woman from her daughter? Atlas's gut knotted. Otis was lower than low.

"May I take a copy of this?" he asked.

"Why would you want to do that?"

"I have some friends who are good at tracking down things. I was thinking they could have a look and see if they can find it for you."

"You don't have to go to that trouble."

"But I'd like to. I'm not sure it's possible to find the locket, but I'd at least like to try."

She shrugged. "Go ahead. But I don't think you'll find it. Trust me, I've tried. For all I know, he threw it in the sea."

Atlas reached out to her, taking her hand in his own. "I'm so sorry you had to go through all of that. You deserve so much better. You deserve someone who loves and cherishes you."

Her eyes shimmered with unshed tears. "You really think so?"

"I do."

"No one has ever said that to me."

When a tear splashed onto her cheek, he moved closer and swiped it away with his thumb. "You should have someone who tells you that you're the most beautiful woman in the world." Their gazes met and held. His heart pounded. "You should be told you have the most alluring eyes that look upon the world with kindness and compassion. And most of all you have the biggest heart."

Another tear splashed onto her cheek. This time she swiped it away. "You don't have to say all of that. It isn't why I told you about Otis."

"I know I didn't have to. I wanted to." It was the truth. He meant every word. "The fact that it's taken me this long to say is my fault."

And then he didn't take the time to weigh the right or the wrong of it. He let himself do what felt right. He leaned toward Hermione, intending to place a kiss upon her cheek. But she turned just as he neared her and his kiss fell upon her lips— her soft, luscious lips.

He should pull away, but he didn't want to. He'd been thinking about her sweet kisses all day. They were addictive.

And then her mouth began to move beneath his. A moan swelled deep down in his throat, and he made no attempt to suppress it. In that moment, he didn't care if Hermione knew how much he wanted her.

There was just something about her that had him acting so out of character—acting like some-one he didn't quite know. With Hermione, he wasn't shut down and cold. She made him open up and feel things. With her, he wanted to take chances and put himself out there.

He thought of the Ruby Heart's legend. Was it possible there was a bit of truth to it? As quickly as the thought came to him, he dismissed it. This thing between Hermione and him wasn't forever. He didn't do commitments.

The next thing he knew, Hermione was pushing him back on the couch. And then her soft curves pressed against him. She started a string of kisses along his jaw that eventually trailed down his neck. His heart beat wildly. How had he become so lucky to have her in his life? And she wasn't looking for a commitment. It would be the perfect holiday fling.

CHAPTER FOURTEEN

SHE AWOKE WITH a smile.

Her hand reached out, finding an empty spot next to her.

Hermione's eyes sprang open. She rolled over and then her gaze searched the room, finding that Atlas was gone. It took her a moment to realize where she was—a guest room in Thea's apartment. They'd moved to the bed sometime during the night—a night in which they hadn't gotten much sleep. Heat rushed to Hermione's cheeks at the memory.

The sun hadn't even risen yet. She couldn't believe she hadn't heard him get up. She yawned and stretched before settling back against the soft pillow, not quite ready to get out of bed and face the day. Atlas must have a lot to do if he was out of bed so early.

She reached for her phone and sent him a text.

Good morning <3

When an immediate response wasn't forthcoming, she scrambled out of bed and headed for the shower. There was no time to waste with Valentine's Day just a few days away.

She was thankful for having had the forethought to bring extra clothes to her office. The very last thing she wanted to do was walk around in yesterday's clothes. That would be a big announcement to everyone that she hadn't gone home last night. And it wouldn't take her friends long to figure out with whom she'd spent the evening. Heat flared in her cheeks as the memories of spending the night in Atlas's arms replayed in her mind.

She took the back way to her office and sneaked inside to switch clothes. Luckily it was so early that even Rhea hadn't arrived yet. Hermione took the opportunity to delegate some tasks to her staff as well as make a minor adjustment to the Valentine's menu.

By the time Hermione completed her emails, the resort was in full swing.

She grabbed her digital notebook so she could start checking off items. As she rushed back to the ballroom, she nearly ran into Adara. "Sorry. It's a busy morning."

"Good morning. Should I ask how things are going?"

She wasn't sure if Adara meant with the party

preparations or between her and Atlas. She opted to go the safe route. "The preparations are on schedule. I just feel like the party needs something else."

"Something as in? The menu? The decorations?"

"That's just it. I don't know. It's just this feeling I have that won't leave me."

Adara sent her a smile. "I'm sure it'll come to you. And how are things with you and Atlas?"

Her body tensed. Their relationship was all so new to the both of them. She wasn't ready to dissect it. She wanted to leave it be for a little longer.

"Things are...are good." She swallowed hard. "Oh, yes, I was supposed to let you know that Atlas's friend, Krystof, has arrived. Atlas is showing him around the resort, but this evening Krystof will require a seat at the high-stakes poker game."

Adara's brows rose. "Does he know that it's a hundred-thousand-dollar buy-in?"

"Atlas said money wasn't an issue."

Adara nodded. "Okay, then. I'll make sure he's on the list."

Hermione gave her Krystof's full name. She didn't know much else about him. The truth of the matter was she'd been too distracted with Atlas as they explored this new facet of their private life to talk about much else. But if Atlas was inviting his friends to the island, that had to mean he was thinking of keeping it.

Adara finished adding the information to her digital notebook. "I'm glad everything is going well with you and Atlas. Let me know if you need anything. I think between the two of us, we might convince him to stay on the island."

Hermione smiled. "I was just thinking the same thing."

"I should be going. I have a meeting with a nervous bride-to-be. If I ever decide to change professions, please remind me that wedding planning is not for me."

Hermione laughed. "It's going that well?"

Adara nodded. "But we'll get through it. And how about you? Are you excited about attending the Valentine's ball?"

Hermione vehemently shook her head. "I'm not going. At least not as a guest."

Adara's eyes reflected her surprise. "But you have to after all the work you put into the preparations. And I know Atlas will be disappointed if you're not there."

Hermione again shook her head. "I can't." She failed to mention that she didn't have a dress for the ball. And she had absolutely no time to shop for one. Plus there was the tiny matter that Atlas hadn't asked her to be his date. "But I'll be working in the background."

Adara studied her for a moment. "Isn't there some way to change your mind?"

"It's for the best. Besides I'd never find anything to wear at this late date." Completely un-comfortable with the conversation, she said, "Can we talk later? I really have to get to the ballroom."

"Don't dismiss the idea of attending the ball. We'll talk more later."

And then Adara was gone. Hermione contin-ued on her way. She knew Adara meant well, but she wasn't going to the ball. She'd have to be content with planning it. Still, why hadn't Atlas mentioned it?

The day had not gone as planned.

This morning's meeting with the photographer for the real estate agent had been agonizingly slow and beyond frustrating. Atlas wasn't good with playing the patient tour guide as the pho-tographer took his time getting the perfect shot.

But the day wasn't a total loss. Krystof had ar-rived. And Atlas had him on the go most of the day. There was so much to see and do at the re-sort. It was concluded with a late dinner at Under the Sea. To Atlas, the restaurant felt as though it were part of a great big aquarium. He thought of it as the highlight of the resort.

As soon as the thought crossed his mind, he realized it wasn't true. Hermione was the true highlight of the resort. She kept the place hum-ming along smoothly. And even when they hit some rough water, such as the problem with the

Valentine's ball, she did what was needed to keep things going.

She was a true leader—a great leader. And if he were to keep the resort, she'd definitely remain the manager and get a large raise.

"What are you smiling about?" Krystof studied him.

He was smiling? He swallowed and assumed a neutral expression. "What do you think of the restaurant?"

"I don't think it's what had you smiling."

He wasn't going to have this conversation with Krystof. He'd make too much of what was going on with him and Hermione. "I was able to get you a seat at the card table tonight."

"Good. I've been looking forward to seeing what the island has to offer."

"I think you'll be impressed." At least Atlas hoped so. "And then we can revisit the idea of you buying this island paradise."

Krystof rested his elbows on the table and leaned forward. "Paradise? Aren't you layering it on a little thick?"

Atlas shook his head. "I don't think so. You can settle down here and soak up some sun when you're not trying your hand with lady luck."

"I don't know. I'm not one to stay in one place for long."

"Trust me. This place is awesome."

"If it's so great, why aren't you keeping it?"

"I probably would if it wasn't a constant reminder of Thea."

Guilt reflected in Krystof's eyes. "Sorry. For a moment, I forgot."

Krystof knew that Thea had abandoned Atlas as a young boy. It was kind of hard to hide when she was never around for any of the school events, but Atlas never went into details.

"Just give the island a chance. It's all I'm asking. And if you want to pass, I'll understand. I have a real estate agent working on a listing. One way or another, this island will cease to be my problem."

"Unless you find a reason to stay."

"Not going to happen." Hermione's face flashed into his mind. "I can't stay."

When they finished their meal, Atlas showed Krystof to the casino and the high rollers room. And then he passed by Hermione's office as well as the event planner's office. She wasn't in either place. A sensation of disappointment settled over him—was it possible he missed her? He wasn't used to missing people. He used to pride himself on not needing anyone.

But he had things he wanted to tell her. And he wanted to hear about her day. There was also that matter of clarifying things between them. Atlas expelled an exasperated sigh. Instead of clarifying things with her last night, he'd succeeded in making things more complicated.

The one thing he had accomplished was he'd sent the picture of Hermione's mother's locket to have a private investigator put out feelers with a reward for its recovery. And he'd had one of the finest jewelers in Athens start working on a replica. He paid extra to have it completed as soon as possible because he'd wanted to give it to Hermione before he left the island. And his departure hopefully wouldn't be too far off—not if he could get Krystof to buy the island.

He took the private elevator to Thea's, er, his apartment and was surprised to find the lights on. "Hermione? Are you here?"

"Back here." Her voice came from one of the bedrooms.

He strolled back the hallway and came to a stop at the doorway of his room—the room where they'd made love last night. But Hermione wasn't alone. There was another older woman standing there next to a table.

He was confused. "What's going on?"

"I have a surprise for you."

"For me? But it's not my birthday."

"Aren't you even curious what it is?"

He hesitated. "What is it?"

"A chocolate massage."

Though the idea was quite tempting, he shook his head. "I don't think so." Then his gaze met the older lady's. "Sorry. No offense."

Hermione approached him. "Look at you.

You're all tense. This will do you good. Trust me."
She clasped her hands together as she pleaded
with her big brown eyes. "Please."

He was quickly learning that he had no defense
when she looked at him that way. "Okay. But you
have to join me."

She shook her head. "I can't."

He reached out for her hand, drawing her close.
In a low voice that melted her insides, he asked,
"Is there a way I can change your mind?"

She hesitated. "I have plans."

He arched a brow. "Should I be insulted? Or
jealous?"

"Neither." She laughed. "It's not that kind of
plan. Adara asked me if I'd meet her this evening."

"To do what?"

"I'm not sure."

After she left, he felt as though the air had been
sucked out of the room. There was just something about being around Hermione that filled
him with a warmth. The thought of returning to
his flat in London no longer appealed to him. He
just wanted to be near Hermione. But he refused
to acknowledge what that meant.

What did Adara want?

Hermione was surprised by her friend's invitation. She'd been unusually mysterious about their
plans for the evening. The only thing she'd said
in the text was that she really needed some help.

Hermione had no time to spare, but she'd make an exception for her best friend. She just couldn't stay late. With only four days until Valentine's, she had so much to do. Her stomach shivered with nerves. She may run the resort, but it was very different work from planning a lavish party.

What if she hadn't ordered enough champagne? What if they didn't schedule enough servers? This list of worries went on and on.

The party had to be spectacular. She needed Atlas to see the resort at its very best. She knew the place and its people were growing on him. A successful party would be the final touch to convince him to step into his inheritance.

Maybe she'd made a mistake by not taking time from her hectic schedule to hunt for a party dress and asking him to the dance. After all, who said the woman had to wait around for the man to extend the invitation. But it was too late now to worry about it.

She would be content to hear the after-party stories and see the photos. But the best part would be if Atlas was happy with the event.

Hermione paused outside Adara's office and knocked.

"Come in."

Hermione opened the door. "Hi. What's going on?"

"I need a little help."

Hermione's gaze took in two glamorous dresses. "These are amazing." She stepped closer to the dresses. "How can I help?"

"I'm having problems deciding on a dress. I was hoping you could help me settle on one for the ball."

Surely she hadn't heard her correctly. "You want me to pick out a dress for you?"

"You sound horrified at the thought."

"No. It's just that I don't know how much help I'll be. I don't wear fancy clothes like these. I'm more of the business casual type."

"They are just material sewn together."

Hermione moved closer to the red and white dresses to have a better look. "Silky, shimmery, sexy material sewn together in the most amazing vintage styles."

Adara laughed. "I take it you like them?"

"Who wouldn't like them? I don't know how you'll pick just one."

"How about you try them on?"

Hermione pressed her hand to her chest. "Me?" When Adara nodded, she asked, "But shouldn't you see how they fit you?"

"I need to see how they look on a person and not on a hanger. It'll help narrow things down for me. Go ahead. I know you want to."

Hermione sent her a hesitant look. "Are you sure?"

"Positive."

She tried on the white one first. She didn't have enough curves to fill it out properly. And it hung much too long for her. She insisted Adara try it on. It fit her perfectly.

While Adara wore the white one and tried to decide if she liked it, Hermione tried on the red gown. It fit her so much better. Since the office lacked a mirror, they took photos of each other in the dresses. In addition, there were sparkly, stunning heels to wear with the dresses.

"You need to wear the red dress to the ball," Adara said.

"I told you I'm not going."

"I remember your excuse being that you didn't have a dress. And now you do."

"What? No. These are your dresses."

"Not if I give you one. Besides, the red one looks far better on you."

Hermione shook her head. "You're just saying that so I'll go."

"I mean it."

"If I did go and I'm not saying I will, I'd have to pay you for the dress and shoes."

"Fine. Now we have to work on getting you a date." Adara's eyes twinkled as she smiled. "You should ask Atlas to go with you."

Hermione's mouth opened to refuse, but she couldn't think of a reason not to ask him. Wordlessly she closed her mouth.

"See," Adara said. "You like the idea."

Hermione knew Adara was once again match-making and she should stop her, but she didn't want to. Instead, she decided it was time to turn things on Adara. "I'll ask Atlas if you ask someone to go with you."

Adara's mouth gaped. It took her a moment to gather herself. "Who would I ask?"

"I'm sure you can find someone." Hermione snapped her fingers as the answer came to her. "Atlas's friend is here. Ask him?"

"He...he probably has a wife or a girlfriend."

"He doesn't. I asked."

Adara looked flustered. "He probably doesn't like dances."

"You won't know until you ask him." When Adara frowned at her, Hermione laughed. "Now you know how it feels. So will you ask him?"

"If that's what it takes to get you to the ball with Atlas, then yes."

With a bottle of wine and a pizza delivered for dinner, it was quite an evening. They talked. They laughed. And they had a great girls' night. She'd miss it dearly if the resort was sold.

Anxious to stop by Atlas's apartment on her way home and tell Atlas about her evening, she told Adara good-night. She might even work up the courage to ask him to the ball. She wondered what his answer would be.

But when she got there, she found his bed-room door open and him draped across the bed as though he'd been meaning to get back up but never made it. She grabbed a throw blanket and tossed it over him before tiptoeing away. Her question would have to wait until another time.

CHAPTER FIFTEEN

TOMORROW WAS VALENTINE'S DAY.

And it was all coming together.

Friday morning, Hermione stood in the center of the ballroom taking in the amazing scene. When they'd started the prep work at the beginning of the week, the room had literally just been four plain walls with a ceiling and floor. There hadn't been anything else in the room. But the last few days had been a blur as this humongous room was brought to life. It was magnificent.

Love Under the Stars. She loved the theme. She wished she could take credit for it, but it was Nestor's idea.

Buzz-buzz.

She glanced at her phone. It was a message from Adara.

Did you ask Atlas yet?

No. Did you ask Krystof?

No.

Ticktock.

Back at you.

Hermione resisted the urge to roll her eyes. Then she turned her thoughts back to the party preparation. She still felt as though something was missing. She gazed around at the positive words displayed in neon lights on the one wall and then onto the wall of glass that opened onto a patio that led to the beach, and finally to another wall with a giant mural of the night sky with a crescent moon and the various astrological signs. As beautiful as it all was, she was certain they were missing something.

She turned to where the refreshments were to be displayed. The chocolate fountain was already assembled. No. It wasn't that. It was...

Ugh! It was right on the edge of her thoughts but when she closed her eyes to focus, there was Atlas's very handsome face. His image was always there, distracting her from her work. When she opened her eyes, he was standing in front of her looking so handsome in a light blue houndstooth button-up with his shirttail untucked and wearing a pair of dark jeans with his boat shoes. He looked totally dreamy.

She blinked, making sure she hadn't imagined

him. But he was still there smiling at her, making her heart go rap-a-tap-tap. "Hi. Did you need something?"

He sent her a sexy smile that made her swoon. "I came to see if you needed a hand. I know this is a lot of work. I've cleared my schedule. All I need you to do is to tell me what needs to be done."

She glanced around, trying to figure out a task for him. But she couldn't think of anything that wasn't already being done.

Then she turned to him. "You could tell me what's missing."

His brows drew together. "Missing?"

She nodded. "I have this feeling I can't shake that something is missing."

He glanced around. "You have all of the food sorted, right?"

She nodded. "And the chocolate fountain is all set to go."

"That sounds good to me."

"Are you serious?" She pressed her hands to her hips. "This is the event of the year. It has to be perfect."

He stepped in front of her. "It will be."

She arched a brow. "How do you know?"

"Because you'll be there, and that's all I need to make my evening perfect."

Her heart rapidly thump-thumped. Heat swirled in her chest and rushed up her neck, warming her cheeks. What was she supposed to say to that?

She opened her mouth, but her mind and mouth were at a disconnect. She wordlessly pressed her lips together.

He stepped closer to her. His gaze met hers as he reached for her. "Would you like a demonstration of what makes a perfect evening?"

She stepped out of his reach. "Atlas, stop." But secretly she didn't want him to stop. She wanted to sneak off with him and spend the rest of the day in his arms. "There's work to be done."

One of the workers approached them. "Hermione, where should the champagne fountain go?"

She swallowed hard, trying to hide the fact that Atlas had totally undermined her train of thought. She turned to the young man. "Um, what did you say?" After the man repeated the question, she instructed him to place it on the opposite end of the buffet from the chocolate fountain. Then she turned to Atlas, who wore an amused smile. "You're not funny. I have a job to do. You can't distract me."

"But it's so fun."

This was the moment she should ask Atlas to the ball. Her stomach shivered with nerves. If he escorted her, it would take their relationship public. It would solidify things between them. But if he turned her down...did that mean he wasn't as into her as she was into him?

She swallowed hard. "Atlas—"

"Hermione, we have a question." Two women

approached her with inquiries about the buffet table. Once more asking Atlas to the ball would have to wait, but she was running out of time. She'd ask him soon, she promised herself.

A few minutes later she returned to Atlas's side. "Sorry about that."

"No problem. After all, you're the star of this production."

"That's it." She just had a light bulb moment. A big smile pulled at her lips.

"What's it?" Confusion reflected in his eyes.

"Stars. That's what's missing. A few years back there was a big wedding and they'd used crystal stars. There were hundreds of them everywhere. We can suspend them from the ceiling and use white twinkle lights to make them sparkle." She was so pleased with herself.

"Do you think you have time for all of that?"

She nodded. "But I have to hurry. I think the stars were put in the storage room. It's so big though that it's going to take me some time to find them."

"Why not send someone else?" Atlas asked.

She glanced around the enormous ballroom. It was abuzz with activity. There were people rushing here and there. People either had their arms full or they were putting something together.

"Everyone is busy. I'll just go. It'll be faster and easier."

Atlas frowned. "Two people can find them quicker than one. I'm coming with you."

Hermione shrugged. "Suit yourself."

Moments later they were in the maintenance elevator that would take them to the lower level. Hermione had to admit that she'd never liked it down here. The first thing she did was prop the heavy metal door open. No way was she getting trapped down here.

She glanced over her shoulder at Atlas. Okay, so maybe getting stuck wouldn't be the worst. After all, they'd have to find some way to pass the time, right? A smile pulled at her lips.

The overhead lights weren't that effective, certainly not to read the labels on the boxes. They located flashlights in the janitor's closet, and then they split up searching the storage room. She took the left side while he went to the right. Row after row of shelving units were lined with cardboard boxes.

Hermione flashed the light on the boxes that were well labeled. However, there wasn't any rhyme or reason to their placement on the shelf. This was going to take them some time—time she didn't have. They had to hurry.

What was happening to him?

He hardly recognized himself anymore.

Atlas had left his team to finish the security system in the gallery on their own so he could help Hermione. That wasn't like him. His business always came first...at least it used to.

In the evenings, he'd been cleaning out Thea's very large apartment, but it was slow work. So much so that he'd had to extend his stay for another week. His mother, to his utter surprise, was the sentimental type—except perhaps when it came to her only child. However, her apartment was filled with all sorts of photos and mementos.

His first reaction had been to toss it all in the nearest dumpster, but he knew the things would mean something to the Ludus staff, who had been thoughtful enough to give the items to Thea. And so he started returning the gifts one at a time.

In the process, he'd gotten to know more of the staff. They were good people with a willingness to give him the benefit of a doubt, even though he'd never visited the resort while Thea was alive. For the most part, they didn't bother him with probing questions. But there were a few of the older employees who greeted him with a raised brow. Even that hadn't been so bad because he understood their confusion. It appeared Thea didn't say much about him beyond her close circle of friends.

Even though he had other tasks requiring his attention, he couldn't abandon Hermione. He knew she was nervous about the party. He was certain with all of the attention she'd given the event that it would be a huge success. So much

so that he'd arranged for the real estate photographer to come back and snap some more
photos.

They really didn't have time to waste meandering around this dusty storage room. There were
so many boxes that he was fairly certain they
weren't going to find the stars. Still he flashed
his light on box after box. St. Patrick's Day. New
Year's. The names of the boxes were everything
but what he needed. They were searching for the
Jericho wedding.

Other than holidays, he'd found the Wilson
wedding, the Smith wedding and about a dozen
other weddings, just not the right one. Where was
it? And how long was Hermione going to persist
in this search?

He sighed as he kept checking one box label
after the next. Bored of this monotonous task, his
mind rewound to his conversation with Krystof
about the ball. Atlas had a policy about avoiding
weddings and dances at all costs, but this was
different. He'd seen how excited Hermione was
about the ball. How could he not be there to support her?

He wondered what she'd say if he asked her
out for Valentine's? The truth of the matter was
that he didn't have any idea of her plans. And he
wouldn't know until he asked her—

"Atlas! I found them." The excitement rang out
in Hermione's voice.

A high-pitched metallic squeak filled the silence. What was she up to now? As he headed to her location, he noticed that she'd found a ladder on wheels. She'd wheeled it over and was already halfway to the top by the time he got there.

As he looked up at her, he noticed she was on the ladder in high heels. "Hermione, you shouldn't be up there. Let me do it."

"Why? You don't think a woman can climb a ladder?" She took the last step to the top little platform.

"No. I think you wore the wrong shoes to be climbing around the storage room."

"It's okay. I'm up here now." She reached for the first box.

"Be careful."

She glanced down at him and smiled. "Are you worried about me?"

Was he? He supposed so. But he wrote it off as general concern, like he'd have for anyone. But with each passing day he was finding that Hermione wasn't just anyone—she was someone special.

"Just pay attention to what you're doing." His voice came out a little gruffer than normal.

"Yes, sir." She smiled down at him again.

He held the ladder, even though the wheel lock was secure. It was the only thing he could do as Hermione pulled box after box and piled them in front of her on the little platform.

"Let me carry them down," he said.

"I've got it." She hooked an arm around the first box and started to back down the ladder.

He stood there with his body tensed and ready to spring into action. But she took one careful step after the next. He was about to take his first easy breath when she was one step from the bottom. Then the tip of her heel caught on a rung. He reached out to her, pulling her and box safely to him.

Her head came to rest on his chest. Nothing had ever felt so right in his life. It was like they were two halves of a whole. She'd shown him that even though his heart was tattered and scarred it was still capable of more emotion than he'd ever dared feel before.

Since their lives collided during the rainstorm, his life had been irrevocably changed. He knew deep down he was never going to be the same man. Hermione had changed him for the better.

Once she regained her balance, she glanced up at him and sent him a sheepish smile. "Oops."

She looked so cute in that moment that he couldn't resist taking the box from her and letting it fall to the floor with a thump. Then he wrapped both arms around her and drew her snugly to his chest.

"What is going to happen to you when I'm not around to catch you?" He stared deep into her eyes, feeling as though he could see his future in them.

The gold flecks in her brown eyes twinkled. "I guess you'll have to stick around just in case I need you."

"And what do you need now?" His voice grew deep and gravelly with desire.

Her arms snaked around his neck as she drew him closer. And then her lips were pressed to his. Oh, yes, that's exactly what he needed too.

Hermione pulled away far too soon. "That should hold you over until later."

"Later? But I want more now."

A soft laugh filled the air. "We have work to do. How about you carry down the rest of the boxes. There are a few more on the shelf. And I'll go find a cart to move these to the ballroom."

She turned and walked away. He was left with the awful thought that one day much too soon, he'd be saying goodbye to her and those delicious kisses. The thought twisted his gut up in a knot.

But what was the alternative? Stay here on Thea's island, living in Thea's resort, in Thea's apartment? No. That was impossible. It wouldn't work. With the constant reminder of the woman who'd rejected him and yet fully embraced the Ludus staff, he would become bitter and it would destroy anything he had with Hermione.

There was another alternative: ask Hermione to leave the island with him. It wasn't ideal because he knew how much she loved it here. But it was an idea that he wasn't so quick to let go of, if it meant a chance to see where things would go with Hermione.

CHAPTER SIXTEEN

It was Valentine's.

The day she'd anxiously awaited.

And yet Hermione was totally bummed. Now that all of the party plans were ready to go, she realized she still hadn't asked Atlas to the dance. She reached for her phone to text him, but she hesitated. This was something she should do in person.

Her memory strayed back to their kiss in the storage room. The memory made her heart thump-thump. That kiss was forever etched upon her mind. It wasn't so much his lips touching hers, it was more the way he looked at her. It was though he too sensed there was something serious growing between them. And it was just the beginning.

Hermione had hit the ground running that morning with no makeup and a messy bun. She headed to the ballroom for the final preparations. Everything must be perfect for tonight.

Speaker system test. *Check*.

Musical acts and comedian. *Check*.

Food and refreshments. *Check*.

Ice sculpture. *Check*.

Twinkle lights and stars. *Check*.

She scanned her checklist one last time. Everything on it had been checked, double-checked and in some cases triple-checked. They were all set for tonight. Her stomach shivered with nerves.

She'd told herself that it'd be okay.

She'd told herself she could deal with it.

But she'd only been lying to herself.

She checked the time. Six o'clock. The party was set to start at seven. Atlas had been sweet to offer her his apartment for her to shower and change into her new red dress instead of having to commute back and forth from her place.

When she stepped into the apartment, Atlas was there. But he wasn't alone. There was another man with him. She recognized him as Atlas's friend Krystof. They both turned to her with a serious expression on their faces.

"Hi. Sorry." Hermione wasn't sure if she should stay or go. "I didn't mean to interrupt."

"Hermione, join us," Atlas said.

The men stood. Introductions were made. She noticed that Atlas didn't introduce her as his girlfriend—in fact, no titles were used. But that was okay. She didn't need a title. They knew what they had growing between them.

"I'm sorry for monopolizing so much of Atlas's time," Krystof said.

Her gaze moved between the two men. She hadn't known they'd spent that much time together, but she was happy that Atlas had a friend here at the resort. It would help him feel more at home.

"Not a problem," Hermione said. "I hope you're enjoying your time on the island."

"So far we've scaled the climbing wall twice, enjoyed the wave pool and visited the spa," Krystof said. "I don't like to sit still. I can only imagine what all we'd have to do if it were summer and the beach was open."

"You'll definitely have to come back in June. We have our annual regatta. Do you have a boat?"

"As a matter of fact, I do."

"Then you should consider entering. The prince of Rydiania enters every year."

"I'm sure you'd enjoy it," Atlas said.

Krystof's eyes widened. "You've attended?"

"Uh, no," Atlas said, "but I've heard a lot about it. Sounds like a good time."

"I'll keep it in mind. But right now, there's a Valentine's ball to attend." Krystof turned to Hermione. "Atlas tells me you've put together a fabulous party—the best in the resort's history."

Heat rushed up her neck and settled in her cheeks. "I don't know if it'll be the best, but I hope everyone will have a wonderful time."

"I'm sure they will." Krystof held out his hand to her. "It was nice to meet you." They shook hands. "But now I have to go because I have a date."

"A date?" Atlas sounded surprised before he smiled and shook his head. "Why am I not surprised?"

So Adara had held up her end of the agreement.

Hermione felt the pressure mounting for her to ask Atlas to the ball. But not in front of Krystof.

Atlas walked Krystof to the elevator. "I'll see you at the party."

"See you there."

Atlas closed the glass door and turned to her. "Looks like you have an admirer."

"Hardly. He was just being nice to me because he's your friend."

"I think you underestimate your beauty. It starts on the inside and glows out, putting people at ease. You're like a ray of sunshine on a cloudy day."

Her gaze strayed to the wall of windows. "But it's dark out now."

He smiled and shook his head. "You know what I mean."

"I do. Thank you for the kind words."

She filled him in on the final details for the party. And he let her know that the new security system was up and running. The conversation was very comfortable, very ordinary as though it were customary for them to fill each other in on their days.

Hermione knew it was now or never if she was going to ask him to the ball. Her heart pounded as her hands grew clammy.

"Will you go to the ball with me?" they asked in unison.

Hermione's mouth gaped as Atlas smiled at her. Had that really happened?

When she gathered herself, she pressed her lips together and swallowed. "Did we just ask each other to the ball?"

"I believe we did."

"Does that mean it's a date?" She needed him to confirm they were having an official date that evening—that they were going to let everyone know they were a couple.

"Yes, it does. Now you better get ready. You don't want to be late for your own party."

Buzz-buzz.

Atlas reached for his phone.

Tonight her very own Prince Charming would be her escort. A smile pulled at her lips. This was going to be the best night ever. And she couldn't help wondering if the Ruby Heart had something to do with it.

Atlas's voice interrupted her musing. "It's Krystof. Something came up and he needs to see me. But I can put him off—"

"No. Go. It must be important. We'll meet up at the ball."

"But this is supposed to be a date."

"It still will be. Now go see what he wants."

"Okay. I'll see you later."

And yet he continued to stand there, looking torn between staying with her and going to his friend. The fact he valued her that much wasn't lost on her. Her heart swelled with...with happiness. She wasn't ready to admit to a deeper feeling—not yet.

CHAPTER SEVENTEEN

HE WANTED TO LINGER.

He longed to be the first to see Hermione all dressed up for the ball.

And yet Atlas had been called away because Krystof said he'd made a decision about buying the island. He'd seen enough and was ready to negotiate. If it were for any other reason, Atlas would have willingly skipped out on the meeting. But he needed to close this chapter of his life—move beyond Thea's long shadow.

First, he needed to change clothes. He'd already showered for the second time that day. He changed into his tux. He'd had it sent via special messenger to the resort. He never anticipated needing it when he'd packed for this trip—it seemed so long ago.

The elevator chimed, alerting him to the fact that they had company. He went to meet their guest.

Adara stepped out of the elevator in a white shimmery gown. "Oh. Hi." She smiled at him. "How are things?"

"Good. How's the wedding coming?"

"It was absolutely lovely. Now that it's over, I had a few minutes to slip away and help Hermione get ready for the party."

He was out of excuses to linger around the apartment. And yet he was still hesitant to leave. This wasn't like him. He used to be the type who didn't let anything stand between him and a meeting.

Business used to be the thing he could count on in his life. It was the one constant. His professional endeavors were what got him out of bed in the morning, what drove him all day long and were the last thing he thought of before he fell asleep at night.

But now, it was Hermione that he rushed out of bed to see in the morning. Her engaging company was what kept him going through this whole trying experience. And it was her image that was the last thing on his mind as he fell asleep at night.

And yet his time at the resort was running out. He just couldn't stay here. And he was torn about asking her to leave with him. He'd witnessed how she fit in here at the resort. Her work fulfilled her, and the people were more than just friends. This was her home and the people were her family. To rip her away from this after all she'd gone through after losing her mother would be so very wrong.

Feeling as though the world were weighing on his shoulders, he left the apartment. As he walked through the resort, memories of his time with Hermione lurked around each corner. When he'd come to the island, he'd never anticipated making memories here. Was he ready to give them up so quickly?

He shoved aside his tormenting thoughts. Right now, he had some negotiating to do with his old friend. Krystof greeted him at the door. Over a couple of bourbons, they haggled back and forth. Coming to a sales agreement was harder than Atlas thought it would be. He said upfront that the Ludus employees would need to retain their jobs for at least six months—including Hermione. Krystof agreed. But Atlas still wasn't ready to shake on it.

Krystof leaned back in his chair and studied him. "You don't want to sell the island, do you?"

"Of course I do," he said with more force than was necessary. "Why else would we be meeting?"

Krystof crossed his arms. "I get the feeling your heart is no longer in it. And if I had to guess, it has something to do with that beautiful manager."

"It does not." *Liar.*

"I don't believe you. You have it bad for her." His friend's eyes lit up as he smiled at him—like he had all of the answers to life. "You're in love."

"I am not." Atlas shot out of his chair and began to pace. His back teeth ground together as his body tensed. He didn't know who he was most upset with at the moment. His friend for having fun pointing out the obvious to him. Or himself for letting things get so out of hand with Hermione.

It would never work between them. He wasn't handsome like Krystof. He didn't have a way with words like his car salesman father, and he didn't have a selfless heart like Hermione.

He was…well, he was unlovable.

It's what he'd been telling himself since he was a kid and his mother left. He'd blamed himself. There was something about him that drove her away, and it kept his father from caring about him. And when Hermione got to know him better, she'd find out she couldn't love him either. He had to put an end to all of this now.

His gaze moved to Krystof. "Do you want to buy the island or not?"

His friend arched a brow. "And you don't care what I do with this place after six months?"

Atlas shook his head because he didn't trust his voice. The truth was that he was more invested in this island than he was willing to admit. But if he were to stay—if he were to keep it—he feared the ghosts of the past would destroy him.

Krystof stood and held out his hand to him. Atlas gripped it.

When they shook, Krystof said, "It's a deal."

Atlas hadn't realized how much time had passed. If they didn't leave now, they'd be late for the ball. And he didn't want to miss this party—

the party that Hermione had worked so hard to put together.

With Krystof next to him, Atlas led the way to the ballroom. Though the party had just started, the room was abuzz with people in black tuxes and glittery dresses. Atlas smiled. He was so happy to see that Hermione's party was off to a successful start.

Neon lights in red and white lit up the wall with inspiring words of hope and love. He glanced toward the grand patio. It was lit up with white candles. While inside, red roses adorned all of the tables as well as bowls of heart-shaped candies with printed messages such as *Be Mine* and *Kiss Me*. But it was the crystal stars and twinkle lights suspended from the ceiling that made the whole room appear magical.

But where was Hermione? His gaze searched the room for her. It was so hard to see with so many people in attendance. She had to be here. But where?

He made his excuses to Krystof, who appeared to be looking around for his date. They'd been so caught up in making a deal for the resort that Atlas hadn't even thought to ask him about his mystery date. It must be the reason for his interest in the resort.

Atlas moved about the room, searching for the woman who made this whole evening possible. And still he couldn't find her. He had a feeling with a room of this size, he might be walking around it all night and still miss her.

He moved to the stage where a world-famous K-pop band was playing dance music. He stood off to the side in order to look out over the crowd. Still, no sign of her.

But then his gaze strayed across to Krystof. And not surprisingly, he wasn't alone. The surprise was the identity of the woman he was dancing with—Adara. Both were smiling and appeared to be having a good time.

He'd be having a good time too if he could find Hermione. He was about to backtrack to the apartment to see if she'd changed her mind about attending the party when in through the entrance came Hermione. His gaze latched on to her and stayed with her.

Her long hair hung past her shoulders in loose curls. On top of her head were curls secured with sparkly pins. But it was the smile on her face that drew him to her. He longed for her to smile like that at him.

He hurried off the stage and headed toward her. He just hoped she didn't get away before he made it through the crowd. With a lot of *pardon me* and *excuse me*, he made it to the entrance.

And there was Hermione in an off-the-shoulder red gown. The fitted bodice was studded with crystals that sparkled. The material gathered at her slim waist and then fell loosely down over her hips and stopped at her heels, which also sparkled with crystals. She was…breathtaking.

She stepped up to him. "Atlas, is everything all right?"

He swallowed hard. "Uh, yes…everything is perfect. You…you are perfect."

Color flooded her cheeks. "I don't know about that."

"I do. I've never seen someone so beautiful." As the color in her cheeks intensified, he rushed on to add, "And this party is amazing. Everyone is having a great time."

"Really?" Her eyes lit up with excitement. "You think so?"

"I do." He held his arm out to her. "Will you dance with me?"

A bright smile lifted her lips. "I'd love to."

He had a feeling his feet were going to be sore by the end of the night because he intended on claiming every dance with her. With their time together drawing to a close, he wanted to make more of those happy memories—memories he would carry close to his heart.

As they danced to a slower tune, he drew her in close. He breathed in the delicate floral scent of her perfume. He would never breathe in that scent without thinking of her. How was he ever going to tell her that the sale of the island was in the works?

CHAPTER EIGHTEEN

THE EVENING FLEW BY.

Atlas couldn't remember being so happy. They'd spent the entire evening together. They were making more of those memories that would keep him warm on those long lonely nights ahead of him.

He needed to tell her about the pending sale of the island, but he hadn't found the right moment. And with nine o'clock approaching, the guests had made their way onto the beach to watch the fireworks that would be set off offshore.

And then the countdown began…

"Ten—nine—eight—"

Atlas joined in the countdown. And he couldn't be happier to have Hermione by his side.

"Seven—six—five—"

Though everything had been a disaster when he'd first arrived on the island, they'd taken a surprising turn for the best. And it was all thanks to Hermione. She'd made his visit an enjoyable event.

"Four—three—two—"

Too bad it was coming to an end. Whereas Valentine's was meant to reaffirm one's love and commitment, this thing between Hermione and him, well, it was an ending. And, oh, how he was going to miss her. More than he'd ever imagined possible.

"One!"

A loud boom thundered around them signaling the beginning of the fireworks. A softer *whoosh* could be heard as the fireworks were launched. A cascade of white and red lights glittered in the black velvet sky.

Another *whoosh* was heard, and a sparkling pink heart filled the sky.

Hermione turned to him. "Isn't it spectacular?"

He stared into her eyes and was immediately drawn in by her boundless happiness. It filled his scarred heart and filled in the cracks and crevices—making him feel whole.

Hermione leaned into him. He reached out to her. And the next thing he knew, they were in each other's arms. His lips claimed hers with a need to remember everything about her. He didn't ever want to forget her or this moment.

Even though he wasn't leaving for another week, he already missed Hermione. He pulled her closer, feeling her soft curves pressed to him. A moan swelled in the back of his throat.

There would never ever be anyone like Hermione.

She was sweet and funny at the same time that she was fiercely independent and stubborn. It was an intoxicating combination. And he longed to hold her in his arms forever and ever because he was in love with her. The thought startled him.

He pulled back. Hermione didn't seem to notice that the world seemed to have shifted. Maybe it was just him. Because loving Hermione meant loving this island, and he couldn't do that. This was Thea's island, not his. Never his.

He couldn't let himself get drawn into a fantasy where Hermione was concerned. His business was waiting on him to hit the road and land other big deals. That's what he could count on— his business.

He glanced over and noticed that Krystof was still talking to Adara. "Krystof and Adara seem to have hit it off."

Hermione arched a brow. "Is he the one you were thinking of selling the island to?"

"I still am. That's the reason I invited him here."

Frown lines etched her eyes and mouth. "I thought you changed your mind."

"You want me to keep this island?" When she nodded, he said, "You don't know what you're asking of me."

"But isn't that what we've been working toward? You've even gotten to know the staff."

"Hermione, you're asking too much of me.

Krystof will do a much better job managing the island than I've done."

"No, he won't. He doesn't have a connection to the island like you do."

She was right. No matter how much he wanted to deny it, he was forever linked to this island via Thea. But not in a good way. Thea chose this life and this island over him. How was he ever supposed to reconcile himself to that fact?

He shook his head. "I'm sorry. I can't do it. This sale is going to happen."

Her eyes grew dark as though a wall had just come down between them. "And that's it? No conversation? No negotiation?"

"This is the way it has to be." It was killing him to say these things. He wanted another option. And even though he knew it was selfish, he said, "Come with me. I can show you the world."

She was quiet for a moment as though giving his suggestion serious consideration. "When we're done seeing the world, I want to come home. I want to come back to Ludus."

He shook his head. "I can't."

Disappointment flashed in her eyes. "Then this is goodbye."

Hermione turned to leave but he reached out to her. His hand caught hers. "Don't go. Not like this."

She turned back to him. Her eyes shimmered with unshed tears. "Do you want me to wait so you can leave first? Because once you sign the sales agreement you'll be leaving and we'll never see each other again. My life is here. My friends are here." She gazed deep into his eyes. "Have you ever stayed in one place long enough to make close friends—friends who have your back and you have theirs?"

The truth was that he'd been moving around since he finished university. Though he had a flat in London, he was forever on the road making deals. With technology he didn't have to be in one place to do his job.

"I have a home in London." His tone was firm. "Everything I care about is there."

"Except me." The pain reflected in her eyes dug at him. "Goodbye, Atlas."

He stood still as she walked away.

He desperately wanted to go after her—to tell her that he'd changed his mind. But he couldn't do that. This island would slowly but surely eat away his soul. Thea's memory lurked in the paint colors, the wall hangings—she was everywhere—reminding him that the people you loved the most were the ones that hurt you the most.

Right now, he was the one doing the hurting. And he hated himself for it. But it was better now than later. Because the longer this went on, the more Hermione would invest herself in him, in them, and he would eventually let her down. It was in his genes.

He wanted to rewind life to that rainy night when their lives had collided. He wanted things to go back to the way they used to be—easy and fun. And then he wanted to slow time so he could savor their moments together. But none of that was possible. He was left with his few precious memories.

CHAPTER NINETEEN

HE'D MADE THE biggest mistake of his life.

Buzz-buzz.

And he had no interest in hearing from anyone.

Bleary-eyed, Atlas stumbled through Sunday morning. He'd barely slept the night before. He kept replaying the scene at the party over and over in his mind. The kiss had been perfect. Hermione had been perfect. And he—well, was broken.

The more he told himself that he'd done what was best for Hermione, the more his heart told him it wasn't true. The reason he'd been fighting his love for her was much more serious. He'd been protecting himself from being rejected yet again.

He loved the lilt of her voice. He loved the way her eyes lit up when she laughed. He loved how she stood up for herself—believed in herself. And most of all, he loved how she cared for others—putting their needs ahead of her own. And sadly he knew he couldn't give her what would make her happy. He couldn't stop moving around and settle here on this island.

He knew Hermione would find someone else to love her—someone who would make her happy— someone who would share her vision for the future. The thought of her with someone else made his stomach churn.

Buzz-buzz.

What was it with his phone that day? Did everyone think he constantly worked? Even on Sunday. Well, he used to be that way, but since he'd been on the island, Hermione had shown him what it was like to have balance in life. It was something he intended to carry on after he left here.

Ring. Ring. Ring.

His gaze moved to the landline phone, but he made no motion to answer it. Obviously whoever wanted him was getting impatient. He should care, really he should, but he didn't. The business and the rush of closing a new deal no longer had a pull over him without Hermione in his life.

He was supposed to meet Krystof to sign the papers this morning. There was no point in putting off the inevitable. Once they were signed, he wouldn't be plagued by the what-ifs that had bothered him all night.

He showered without bothering to shave. He dressed but in jeans and a dress shirt that he didn't bother to tuck in. He didn't feel the compulsion to worry about his casual appearance. It was what it was.

Ding-dong. Ding-dong.

He thought of ignoring the private elevator too, but the fact that he needed it to go to a meeting made that impossible. With a resigned sigh, he headed for the intercom and pressed the button to allow whoever it was up to the apartment. A moment later the elevator door slid open, and Adara stood there with her fine brows knitted together in a frown.

"I've been trying to reach you," she said.

"We weren't supposed to meet, were we?"

"No." She crossed her arms. "But we need to talk."

"I'm not really in a chatty mood—"

"This is important." Her firm tone brooked no argument.

He gestured for her to step into the living room. "Give me a second." He strode over to the bar and retrieved a water. "Can I get you anything?"

She perched on the edge of the couch. "No. Thank you."

He sat down on the chair and turned to her. "What do you need?"

"Krystof's counsel has arrived. There's some question as to the ownership of the resort. They want to know if you have a copy of the will."

"Uh…no. I didn't think I'd need it. My attorney assured me that all of the paperwork had been properly filed."

"I believe you. I just think the gentlemen in the meeting room would feel better if they could see verification."

He didn't want to do it. He didn't want to have to deal with Thea's will…again. "I guess the sale will have to be delayed."

"Maybe not."

He arched a brow. "What do you have in mind?"

"Thea, Hermione and I had become very close over the years. She told us if there were any problems that she'd placed a copy of her will in her safe."

"She told you that?"

"Yes. It was after your stepfather passed on. She wanted to make sure the resort went on as it always had and the employees didn't lose their jobs."

He shook his head in disbelief. "If it means ending this sooner rather than later, I'll go check her safe."

And with that he walked away. In the hallway his strides were long and quick. He'd had it with Thea pulling his strings from beyond the grave. He just wanted his life back the way it was supposed to be—where he was in control. It couldn't happen soon enough. Because being here—being without Hermione—was killing him.

By the time he reached Thea's bedroom and removed the large painting from the wall to reveal the wall safe, he was in a perfectly awful mood. He pulled up the code to the safe from the note he'd made on his phone.

The first time he moved the tumbler too rashly and it didn't work. He took a deep breath and blew it out. And then with a steadier hand, he tried once more. This time the safe opened.

He hadn't explored the safe yet. The truth was that he'd been putting it off. He'd been ignoring Thea's entire bedroom. It was just too personal.

The safe was filled with jewelry boxes. None of that interested him. He scanned the safe, looking for the will. As soon as he got it, he was out of there. He was half inclined to tell Adara to do what she wanted with the rest of Thea's belongings since they'd been friends.

On the top shelf of the safe were some papers. He pulled them out. One by one he glanced at them, looking for the will. And then he happened upon an envelope with his name handwritten on it.

He froze. Why would this be in the safe? And then he realized it must be a copy of the will. Since he was the sole heir, it would make sense to have his name on it. Though the envelope did seem a bit slim for such a document.

He opened the envelope, expecting to find some

sort of legal document. Instead, what he found was blue stationery with Thea's handwriting.

> *My dear Atlas,*
> *If you're reading this it means my worst fear has happened. I have died without us reconciling. And for that I am so deeply sorry.*
> *First, I love you. I've always loved you. You are a piece of me—the best part of me.*
> *But I am human, and I made huge mistakes—mistakes I wish I could undo. I never meant to leave you. I swear. I left because I didn't have any other choice. Your father and I couldn't live together any longer. I'll spare you the details but please believe me when I say it was bad, very bad.*

Atlas stopped reading. He wasn't going to let Thea rewrite the past. No way. He was there. He knew what happened.

He tossed the letter aside. He continued his search for the will. That was the reason he was here—the only reason. He wasn't going to give Thea's words any power over him.

He reached back inside the safe and pulled out another stack of stuff. This time there was a book of some sort. Surely the will wouldn't be in there, but curiosity got the best of him and he lifted the other papers off the big bound book. He opened it to find a baby photo of himself.

A voice in his head said to close it and move on, but apparently his body wasn't listening to his mind because the next thing he knew, he was turning the page. Again there were pictures of him as a little boy. Why would she still have these after all of this time?

He turned page after page, finding photos he'd never seen before. His father wasn't big on family photos. But some of these photos were of him and Thea. She was smiling as she cheered him on to blow out candles on his birthday cake. There were others of them at the park.

Page by page, he aged in the photos until they suddenly stopped. And then there were media releases about his company—about him. She'd followed his career from his small start-up company to becoming one of the largest security firms in the world. She had press clippings in here that he'd never seen before.

And then something splashed onto the page. Luckily there was a clear plastic sheath over the clippings so he could wipe away the moisture without it damaging anything. And then there was a drip on his hand. He lifted his fingertips to his cheek and realized the moisture was coming from him.

He swiped at his cheeks as he continued flipping through the pages. Thea had followed his life right up until she'd died. Why would she do that if she didn't care about him?

He set aside the scrapbook and reached for Thea's letter once more. He continued reading as she explained that his father had physically thrown her out. With his father being much older than Thea, he'd had a lot of power over her. He'd threatened that if she ever tried to see Atlas again that both she and Atlas would pay for it. At the time she'd been too poor to fight him in court as he owned a car dealership and had many resources and lots of influential connections in the community.

It wasn't until she met Georgios and fell in love that she was able to fight his father. She went back for Atlas but by then he had been swayed by his father into thinking that she'd willingly abandoned him. He'd wanted nothing to do with her.

She went on to explain that she didn't know what to do. She didn't want to make things worse for him so she left. But she never stopped loving him.

She left him this island because it's where she healed and flourished. She'd hope it would bring him happiness and love. He rubbed his eyes and read the letter again.

All of this time, he'd thought his mother hadn't loved him. And maybe she hadn't handled the situation the way he would have liked, but she did the best she could. No one was perfect, most especially not him.

And that was the reason he'd been holding himself back from picturing a future with Hermione. But the truth was that he couldn't imagine his future without her.

If he left the island now, would he be following in his mother's footsteps? Would he be walking away from the chance to give love and be loved? Shouldn't a lesson be learned from what happened with him and his mother? Sometimes people weren't given second chances—sometimes you had to seize the moment.

Atlas set aside the letter. He had to find Hermione. And he had to find her right now. No, he needed to pause in order to form a plan—proof that he loved her.

CHAPTER TWENTY

A WEEK OFF from work.

Monday morning, Hermione looked around her modest flat and couldn't find a thing she felt like doing. And yet she couldn't go back to the Ludus—not yet. She had a lot of unused time off, and now was the time to use some of it.

In a week, Atlas should have his business wrapped up at the resort. She pushed the painful thought of him to the back of her mind. She supposed she should be happy he hadn't fired her.

How had she ever let herself get caught up in the legend of the Ruby Heart? She blamed it for letting herself fall hard for Atlas and believing that he could change. She had been so foolish.

She needed to stay busy. Her gaze moved around the bedroom. Her bed was already made up without a wrinkle. Everything was in its place. And it all felt so empty.

She told herself it had nothing to do with Atlas—nothing to do with the fact that he'd soon be flying back to London, nothing to do with the fact that she would never again lay eyes on him.

She retraced her steps to the living room. Her heart ached as she pictured his handsome face. She reached for an old faded throw pillow on the couch and hugged it to her chest. Then just as quickly she tossed aside the pillow. She was not going to sit around feeling sorry for herself. She was fine before Atlas and she'd be fine after him.

She moved to the two houseplants she'd bought yesterday at the market. She'd given them names. One was Spike and the other Ivy. Not original names, but she liked them.

She gave them each a drink of water and placed them on the windowsill to soak up some sunshine. She glanced around for something else to do—something that needed her attention. Perhaps she should adopt a dog. Then again, when she went back to work, she wouldn't be home much. Perhaps a cat would be better. She liked the idea. It would be nice to have someone to come home to. Then Atlas's image once more appeared in her mind. She exhaled a deep sigh. How could she have read things so wrong between them?

Knock-knock.

It was probably her neighbor, Mrs. Persopoulos. She was very sweet. And Hermione tried to help her out by carrying her groceries up the stairs or helping to clean her tiny apartment when she was available.

Hermione moved across the flat in just a few steps. She forced a smile to her face as she opened the door, only to find it wasn't Mrs. Persopoulos. There was a delivery person holding a bouquet of red roses.

"Ms. Kappas?"

"Yes."

"These are for you." He held the arrangement out to her.

She automatically accepted them. "Thank you."

Her heart raced. No one had ever sent her flowers—certainly not her ex. Could these be from Atlas? No. Of course not. Why would he send her flowers?

She rushed to her small table and placed the vase of flowers atop it. There was a note attached. She pulled the card from the envelope.

I'm sorry!
Atlas

They were from him. Her breath caught in her throat. What did that mean? He was sorry for what? Hurting her? Walking away?

The questions continued to roll around in her mind. Hope began to swell in her chest. She knew that was dangerous. She didn't want to get her heart broken. But wasn't it already broken?

Because she loved Atlas, even if he didn't love her in return.

She leaned over and inhaled the flowers' delicate scent. She had to know what this was all about; she reached for her phone. Her hand had a slight tremor as she dialed Atlas's phone.

It rang once. Twice. Three times.

Knock-knock.

She rushed to the door and swung it open. There stood another delivery person. "Ms. Kappas?"

"Yes." This was beginning to take on a sense of déjà vu.

He held out a small brown-paper-wrapped package. She thanked him and closed the door. She moved to the couch and sat down. What was it this time? She assumed it was also from Atlas. Why was he showering her with gifts?

She tore off the paper to find a box of specialty chocolates and an envelope. She opened it, finding a gift certificate for a chocolate massage at the resort's spa. And a note in Atlas's handwriting.

I know how much you love chocolate. I hope you will enjoy these and maybe you will find it in your heart to forgive me. Please. Perhaps a chocolate massage will help. I know I enjoyed the one you planned

*for me. You are so thoughtful—so kind. And
I miss you!*

Hermione read the message again. And again.
What was he trying to tell her? Had he changed
his mind about keeping the island—about their
relationship?

Knock-knock.

CHAPTER TWENTY-ONE

HE WAS TAKING a chance.

This was a risk he'd never taken in his life.

In the past, when a woman was tired of his workaholic and nomadic ways, she walked away. He never followed—never asked for a second chance. And yet with Hermione, he was willing to risk it all—his pride and most of all…his heart—if it meant a chance for him to win her back.

He'd done a lot of soul-searching over the past two days since she'd left, and he knew his life just wasn't the same without her in it. But would he be able to convince her to give him a second chance?

His heart thump-thumped as he knocked on her door. He braced himself for the possibility of having the door slammed in his face. He wouldn't blame her. He'd made an utter mess of things.

Each second dragged on. And then he heard footsteps and the door swung open. Hermione looked adorable in her blue jeans and pink cotton top. Her long hair was swept back in a ponytail. And there wasn't a trace of makeup on her face—not that she needed any. She had a natural beauty about her. But he did notice the shadows beneath her eyes.

"Atlas, what are you doing here?"

"I'm hoping you'll come somewhere with me."

"I... I don't know." She worried her bottom lip. "Where?"

He noticed she didn't invite him inside. "Back to the beginning."

"What beginning?"

"Ours." His gaze searched hers. "Please."

There was a moment of silence as though she were deciding what she should do. All the while, he willed her to agree. He wanted so badly to make things right between them.

"Okay." Her voice was so soft that for a moment he thought he'd imagined it. "Let me grab my stuff."

A moment later she had on a light jacket, white tennis shoes and a gray purse slung over her shoulder. He led her downstairs and outside to his one-of-a-kind black sports car. As he zipped along the streets, she peppered him with questions but he held her off.

He wanted to do this right.

And so he distracted her with talk of the warm weather and trivial matters. The fact they were communicating on any level he took as a positive sign. Soon they arrived at the dock. A short ferry ride and they were on Ludus Island. He navigated the car along the winding road until they came to the spot of the accident. He pulled to the side of the road and turned off the engine.

"What are we doing here?" Hermione asked.

He got out but when he rounded the front of the car to open the door for her, she was already exiting the vehicle. "I thought we should go back to the beginning of you and me."

"You meant it literally." She gazed around.

"Signs of the accident have all been washed away with the flooding rains, but one thing wasn't, the initial feelings I had for you. They've only grown since I've gotten to know you."

She eyed him suspiciously. "The only thing you felt for me that night was anger."

He shook his head. "I'm sorry I was so grouchy in the beginning, but you didn't let it run you off. You stood your ground and made me see sense during one of the darkest times of my life. You're the strongest woman I know. And I'm so much better off by knowing you."

Her eyes shimmered with unshed tears. She blinked repeatedly. "You really think I'm strong?"

Once more he nodded. "So much stronger than me because you were willing to admit that what we had wasn't just a holiday fling—it was so much more. But I was afraid to put my heart on the line—afraid I wasn't worthy of your love."

She reached out to him, cupping his cheek with her hand. "How could you think that? You are amazing and sweet. Any woman would be lucky to have you in their life."

He leaned down and pressed his lips to hers. The kiss was short. He didn't want to get distracted. He needed to get this all out there. He needed to fix what he had broken.

Summoning all of his strength and determination, he pulled away from her sweet kiss. Her eyes fluttered open and stared at him with confusion reflected in her eyes.

Her heart raced.

Hermione could hardly believe she was here with Atlas and that he was kissing her. Hope and excitement swelled within her, but she refused to let it take over. She had to know that Atlas was fully invested in their relationship. She had to hear him say the words.

She loved him, but she wasn't going to make this easy for him. She wasn't going to assume what he meant by this grand gesture. If he was going to be in this for the long haul with her, he had to be willing to put himself out there—the whole way.

"Why did you bring me here?" she asked.

"I told you, so we could start over. Come back to the resort."

"You mean to continue running the place until the new management can take over?"

He shook his head. "There isn't going to be any new management."

She was confused. "There isn't?"

"Krystof and my mother helped me see that this place, this island—and you are my future. That is if you still want me."

Oh, boy, did she ever. It would be like a dream come true. Wait. Had she heard correctly? "Your mother?"

He nodded and explained about the letter and the scrapbook. "I just wish she'd have reached out again and that I would have been mature enough to hear her out." His gaze searched hers. "I don't want to repeat my mother's mistake and walk away from someone I love. Will you give me another chance?"

A tear splashed on her cheek. "You love me?"

He held up a finger for her to wait a moment. Then he reached in his suit jacket and pulled out a black velvet box. Her heart leaped into her throat.

"Go ahead," he said. "It's for you."

Another gift? The gifts were really sweet. He was trying really hard to get this right. She accepted the box and opened it. Inside was a locket. The breath hitched in her lungs. She knew this locket. She looked closer. It looked so much like her mother's missing locket.

"It's not the original," Atlas said. "I had a duplicate made until we can recover the original."

No one had ever done something so thoughtful for her. She lifted her gaze to his. "Thank you for being so sweet."

"Open it."

She swiped at her cheeks and then she did as he asked. Inside were two little heart-shaped pieces of paper with the words *I love you* written on them.

Her gaze lifted to his. "You do?"

He nodded. "With all of my heart."

And then she had the most incredible realization. "It's true."

"What's true?"

"The legend of the Ruby Heart."

"Is it?" His gaze challenged her. "Will you come back to the resort with me?"

She smiled and nodded. "I love you too." But then she realized that she now had other responsibilities. "But can Spike and Ivy come with me?"

"Spike and Ivy?" He shrugged. "Bring whoever you want. My home is your home."

"Good. Because I've kept those houseplants alive for two days now and I'd hate for anything to happen to them."

He laughed and shook his head. "Maybe we should think about getting you a dog."

"Or a cat."

"Or one of each." He pulled her close. "I've always been a bit of a nomad, but I can't wait to set down roots with you. And Spike and Ivy."

"Before we do that, how about we do some more of this?" She lifted up on her tiptoes and pressed her lips to his.

EPILOGUE

Four months later... Ludus Island

EVERYTHING WAS LOOKING UP.

The resort was bustling with sunseekers.

And Hermione had never been happier in her life.

Right now, she was gearing up for the resort's biggest event of the year—the Royal Regatta. It was due to kick off tomorrow, and Hermione was a nervous wreck. Everything had to go perfectly with Prince Istvan of Rydiania in attendance.

Additional staff had been hired to make this year's regatta bigger and better than ever. Nestor was back at work, seeing to all of the event's details. While Atlas was splitting his time between his security business and running the resort. He was very busy, but Hermione had never seen him happier. And that filled her heart with joy.

Hermione stood outside on the veranda taking in the view of smiling guests enjoying the beach.

June was her favorite time of the year. There was an energy that flowed through the resort—

"Excuse me, Miss Kappas. Where do you want me to set up?"

Hermione turned to their latest hire. She searched her memory for the young woman's name. It took Hermione a second to recall it. "Good morning, Indigo. We're so happy to have you as part of the Ludus family. I've had a large umbrella set up for you on the beach. Just let us know what else you need—"

"Good morning, Hermione." The deep male voice had a distinct foreign accent.

Hermione would know that sexy voice anywhere. She immediately turned and then curtsied. "Your Royal Highness."

He smiled. "Hermione, I told you curtsying isn't necessary."

"But it feels wrong not to. After all, you're a prince."

"Don't remind me. I have those guys to constantly remind me." He gestured over his shoulder to the small army of dark suited men with sunglasses and earpieces. His gaze moved to Indigo. His smile broadened. "And who might you be?"

Hermione noticed how the young woman's eyes widened. When Indigo appeared to be shocked into silence, Hermione intervened. "This is Indigo. She's a talented artist."

"Is that so?" The prince's gaze studied the woman. "A beautiful artist."

If Hermione didn't know better, she'd think the prince was drawn to Indigo. But he was normally smooth and flirtatious with all of the pretty ladies. This meeting was no different. Or was it? "Perhaps she could do a sketch for you."

"I'd like that." He was still staring at Indigo, who was now blushing. "But it'll have to wait. I have some business to attend to." He turned his attention to Hermione. "I wanted to say hello and find out how things are going now that Thea's son owns the island."

"Things are going well." She smiled as she thought of Atlas. "Very well. I'll have to introduce you to him."

"I'd like that. Now I must be going." He gave Hermione's hand a butterfly kiss. And then he did the same for Indigo. "I look forward to our next meeting."

After he was gone, Indigo still hadn't spoken a word. Hermione couldn't blame her. The prince was quite charming. And then there was that sexy accent.

"You can go set up," Hermione said, jarring the woman out of her stupor.

"I… I can't believe I didn't say a word to him."

Hermione smiled. "It's fine. I'm sure he's used to it."

Once Indigo moved on, Hermione checked her

email on her digital tablet. She should be in her office working, but the sunshine and sea breeze had called to her. She'd have to go inside soon, but she just needed a minute or two more of fresh air.

"Here you are." Atlas stepped up next to her. "Are you busy?"

"I'm never too busy for you." She lifted up on her tiptoes, pressing her lips to his. When she pulled away, she asked, "What do you need?"

"More of those kisses." He smiled at her.

"I'm afraid you'll have to wait until later."

He sighed. "In that case, I need you to come see something."

"Please tell me nothing's wrong. The prince just arrived. Oh, and he wants to meet you."

He arched a brow. "Should I be jealous that you're buddies with a prince?"

"No. I already have my prince." She gave him another quick kiss. "Now what's going on? Is it the security system?" She followed him inside to the elevator. "We assured the prince that everything was now state of the art."

"It's not the security system." He pressed the down button.

"We're going to the Under the Sea restaurant?"

Atlas turned to her. He cupped her face in his hands. "Stop worrying. I promise you everything is going to be perfect."

"But you said I had to see something."

"I didn't say it was something bad. Did I?"

"But—"

He leaned over and pressed his lips to hers. Immediately her stress started to dissipate. She leaned into him and returned the kiss. She would never ever get tired of kissing him.

The elevator dinged as the door slid open. With great reluctance, she pulled away from Atlas. But he in turn took her hand in his.

"Come on." He led her past the waiting area.

The restaurant was only open for dinner service so with this being noon, it should be empty. But when they stepped into the dining room, there was a table in the middle of the room. There was a few candles and a huge bouquet of red roses.

Hermione turned to Atlas. "I don't understand."

He smiled. "I have a surprise for you." He drew her closer to the table that was set for lunch—a champagne lunch. He picked up a black velvet box. He held it out to her. "This is for you."

She smiled. "You have to quit spoiling me."

"But I enjoy it. I love making you smile."

She opened the box. Inside was a locket, exactly like the one she was wearing. "You got me another locket?"

"No. I got you the real locket—your mother's locket."

"You found it!" Tears rushed to her eyes as her finger traced over it. "I never thought I'd see it again." Her watery gaze moved to his. "Thank you."

"Open it."

This definitely felt like déjà vu. But she did what he said. Inside, resting on top of the photos of her parents, were two little pieces of paper.

On the left it said: *Will you...*

The right read: *...marry me?*

She read it twice, just to make sure she'd read it correctly. When she looked at Atlas, she found him on bended knee. He held out a smaller black velvet box with a big beautiful emerald cut diamond ring.

"Hermione, I fell for you from the first time I saw you. I didn't need a ruby to tell me how special you are. I just had no idea how much you would change my life for the better, and now I can't imagine my life without you in it. Will you marry me?"

By now the tears of joy had rolled onto her cheeks. Her heart went pitter-patter with love. "Yes. Yes, I'll marry you."

He straightened, slipped the ring on her finger and then pulled her into his arms, claiming her lips with his own. She had found the love of her life. How had she gotten so lucky?

* * * * *

*Look out for the next story in
the Greek Paradise Escape trilogy.
Coming soon!*

*And if you enjoyed this story,
check out these other great reads from
Jennifer Faye*

Falling for Her Convenient Groom
Bound by a Ring and a Secret
Fairytale Christmas with the Millionaire

All available now!